SAM'S SURRENDER

HEARTS & HEROES SERIES BOOK #4

ELLE JAMES

TWISTED PAGE INC

SAM'S SURRENDER

HEARTS & HEROES SERIES BOOK #4

New York Times & USA Today
Bestselling Author

ELLE JAMES

eBook ISBN-13: 978-1-62695-085-6

Print ISBN: 978-1-62695-086-3

This book is dedicated to my mother and father who encouraged me to follow my dreams and to work hard to make them happen. I love you both so very much.

AUTHOR'S NOTE

Enjoy other military books by Elle James

Hearts & Heroes Series
Wyatt's War (#1)
Mack's Witness (#2)
Ronin's Return (#3)
Sam's Surrender (#4)
Brotherhood Protector Series
Montana SEAL (#1)
Bride Protector SEAL (#2)
Montana D-Force (#3)
Cowboy D-Force (#4)
Montana Ranger (#5)
Montana Dog Soldier (#6)
Montana SEAL Daddy (#7)
Montana Ranger's Wedding Vow (#8)
Montana Rescue

Visit ellejames.com for more information
For hot cowboys, visit her alter ego Myla Jackson at
mylajackson.com
and join Elle James and Myla Jackson's Newsletter at
http://ellejames.com/ElleContact.htm

SAM STARED down at the Thira Airport landing strip on the Greek island of Santorini, his fingers biting into the armrest of his airline seat.

In the air, he preferred to be the pilot, and that the aircraft be the Blackhawk he flew for the Army. In fact, he'd rather be with his unit, the 160th Night Stalkers, ferrying Special Operations teams to the hot spots of Afghanistan, Iraq and Syria, than at the mercy of an island-hopping, fixed-wing pilot who got his flight status from a cereal box. Based on the hard landing, Sam wondered how many hours the pilot had under his belt, or if he'd ever been in the Navy performing landings on an aircraft carrier.

The thought of spending two weeks staring at the crystal-clear waters of the Mediterranean Sea and the shockingly white buildings of his vacation location made his teeth grind. What the hell was he going to do for the entire time? The inactivity would make him batshit crazy. He lived for his team, for the Army, and for the next mission.

His commander called him an adrenaline junkie, always looking for his next high. Maybe Colonel Cooley was right. So what? Someone had to pilot the helicopters into and out of war-torn areas.

Sam didn't have a wife and kids to go home to. Why not let him ferry in the real bad-asses to complete their missions?

His commander's response had been, "Magnus, you're pushing the limits, getting too close and scaring the crap out of your passengers."

"And the fact they're going into firefights isn't frightening enough?"

The CO pointed a stiff finger at him. "Exactly. Those Spec Ops dudes have enough on their minds. They don't need some rotor-head making them upchuck before they have to sling bullets at the enemy."

"That SEAL shouldn't have been on my bird. He had the flu."

"The flu, hell. You were popping in and out of those hills like a prairie dog in heat. What did you expect those guys to do? Half of them were hurling chunks. The point is, you're taking risks and not keeping the souls on board in mind while you're doing it." Colonel Cooley pushed back from his desk and stood. "Flying is not all about you. It's about the goddamn mission."

Sam stood in front of the CO at attention, taking his chewing out. Yeah, he probably deserved it. But hell, he was the best pilot in the unit. He could fly circles inside the circles around the other Black Hawk pilots. He tried to calm his commander by stating, "Sir, I promise to do better."

"Damn right, you will. But that's not enough. Other members of the unit, and I, have noticed you're wound entirely too tight. If you don't learn to relax, you'll explode like forty pounds of C4."

"Sir, I'll take it easy."

The colonel's lips formed a thin, tight line. "Yeah." The CO resumed his seat behind the metal desk. "You're scheduled for leave starting tomorrow, correct?"

"Yes, sir," he said. "I'm attending my brother's wedding in Ireland. I'll be gone four days, max."

"Wrong."

Sam's head jerked back. "Sir?" He stared at his commander, a frown narrowing his eyes. "I had this leave approved months ago. But if you can't spare me, I'll call and tell Wyatt I can't make it."

"I didn't say you weren't getting your leave. You're attending your brother's wedding, and then you're taking an additional two weeks of leave to chill out, wind down and fucking get a grip on your nerves, your attitude and your life."

His stomach lurched as if he'd been sucker punched. "But, sir, I'm needed here. I'm the best damn pilot you've got."

Colonel Cooley shook his head, his lips twisting into a frown. "You might have the best skills, but right now, you're a loose cannon, and a danger to yourself and the people you're supposed to be helping."

"You can't be serious," Sam raised both hands. "I

haven't taken that much time off in years. I wouldn't know what to do with myself."

The CO glanced up at him without speaking for a full thirty seconds.

Sam began to sweat. Even he knew he'd crossed the line, questioning his superior officer's judgment. He clamped his lips tight and waited for the additional ass-chewing to come.

"I'm as serious as a heart attack. And, if I'd been in the chopper on your last flight, I might have *had* a heart attack."

When Sam opened his mouth, the CO held up his hand to stop him.

"If two weeks' leave isn't enough to get your head on straight, I'll have to ground your ass. Don't make me to it."

Sam's gut clenched. Ground him? That would be a fate worse than death. What would he do if he couldn't fly? Flying was his life. Flying defined him.

Too shocked to say another word, Sam stood like a stone statue.

"Get out of my sight for two weeks and four days. When you return, I'll determine whether or not you're ready to fly again. I suggest you take the time to get your shit together. Go for a walk, find a beach, get laid, meditate…whatever you need to do to figure out how to calm down." He waved toward the door. "Now, get the hell out of my office."

Sam popped a salute, executed a sharp about-face and marched out of the office.

That had been five days ago. He'd been to Ireland for

his brother Wyatt's wedding, which had ended up being more stressful than flying into enemy territory. His brother Mack's girl had been targeted by Irish gypsies after she witnessed one of them murder another guest in the wedding hotel.

The visit turned into a nightmare. For a while there, Mack and his sweetheart had been touch-and-go in a ploy to flush out the Travelers and squelch their attempt to kill them.

What had happened in Ireland had not made for a good start to his enforced R&R.

The pilot taxied the airplane to the terminal and stopped.

As soon as the seatbelt sign blinked off, Sam punched the release on the metal buckle, stood and grabbed his go bag from the overhead bin.

And waited, tapping his fingers on the back of the chair in front of him. The sooner he was off the plane and on terra firma, the quicker this nuisance of a vacation could begin. Today was D minus fourteen.

The ground crew took what felt like forever to push a flight of stairs up to the fuselage, but finally, the cabin door was open and the passengers filed out.

The setting sun glared into Sam's eyes and a salt breeze ruffled his hair. He blinked and shaded his face until he entered the terminal. Again, time dragged until he cleared customs. He kept his military ID tucked away in his wallet. No use alerting anyone to American military in the area. Terrorists existed in every corner of the world. As the crow flew, Santorini wasn't that far from the troubles plaguing the Middle East.

He'd booked a bed and breakfast room on a hilltop overlooking the whitewashed city. From looking at the map, he gauged the distance was a good walk, mostly uphill, from the airport. He could use the exercise and decided to skip a taxi and stretch his legs.

The sun slipped into the ocean as he slung his bag over his shoulder and set off at a quick pace, inhaling the salty air and wondering what activities were available on a dinky-shit island.

He should have stayed on the mainland of Europe where he could hop a train to anywhere he wanted. But no, the dart had to land on Santorini. Perhaps his method of picking destinations was flawed.

Maybe he'd find a bar and drink himself into oblivion for the next two weeks. What else was there to do?

KINSEY PHILLIPS HAD SPENT her day off snorkeling in one of the many picturesque coves Santorini had to offer. The au pair gig she'd landed came at the perfect time and, so far, the job wasn't hard at all.

The Martins had been nice, if a little stand-offish, and their two children were well-behaved and quiet. Kinsey tried to get them to open up, but she figured she was still too much of a stranger for the kids to trust her.

She wasn't too worried. The family was supposed to be on Santorini for a full month. That would give them time to get to know her. By the end of the month, they'd love her and beg to keep her on as their permanent nanny.

And, if a month was all she had, at least she'd earn enough money to purchase her plane ticket back to the States.

Her first time in Europe had been nothing if not fraught with drama, but everything seemed to be working out. Finally.

She'd sold all her furniture, emptied her bank account, pulled up all her stakes and moved to Greece to take a job as an assistant manager of a hotel in Athens. With a one-way ticket, she'd boarded a 777 and left her crappy love life behind.

Her heart full of dreams and hope for the future, she'd landed, eager to start her new job and try her skills at speaking Greek.

The job had fallen through upon arrival. The hotel had been bought out by a competitor, and she'd been let go before she even started. Not too deterred, she'd decided to spend a couple weeks in Athens, maybe find another job or just enjoy a short vacation. Two days into her stay, she was mugged. Thieves had taken her backpack with everything inside—her money, laptop, cellphone, passport and credit cards.

She had no parents to call and bail her out, or friends she could count on back in Virginia. In her last job, she'd been the secretary to an elderly gentleman who had retired and moved to Cabo San Lucas. Kinsey had no backup.

Broke, with no way to pay for her room, food, a plane ticket home or even a phone call, she'd sat on a bus bench and cried.

That's when Lois Martin sat beside her and quietly asked what was wrong.

Kinsey had been so happy to hear someone speak English, she'd poured out her troubles to the stranger.

An hour later, she had a job offer, a plane ticket to Santorini and a taxi ride to the U.S. Embassy to get a replacement passport. In just that short amount of time, her life was back on track.

Now that she'd been in Santorini for a week, she was beginning to feel downright optimistic. She smiled as she climbed the hill to the hotel where she and the Martins were staying and where she occupied the adjoining room next to their suite.

The concierge nodded as Kinsey entered the hotel. "Good evening, Miss Phillips. I have a message for you." He handed her a sealed envelope.

The Martins often left notes for her at the concierge, informing her of their dinner plans and whether she should join them. "Thank you, Giorgio." She tore open the envelope and slipped free the note card. "Did you get to see that sunset? It was beautiful."

"Haven't been outside the hotel since I got here this morning."

"Such a shame. But then, I imagine all the sunsets are as pretty here on Santorini." She glanced down at the card. *Meet us at the Naousso Café at eight.* "What time is it?" she asked.

"Fifteen minutes to eight o'clock," he replied.

Her heart skipped a beat. She didn't have much time to change and get to the restaurant. "I'd better get going."

"I'm glad you've enjoyed your stay," Giorgio said. "Will you be leaving soon, as well?"

Why would he ask if she was leaving? When she'd told him a week ago that she'd be there for a month. "No, I'll be here for another three weeks."

The concierge frowned and opened his mouth to say something, but a woman approached him with questions about nearby restaurants.

Kinsey smiled, waved and stepped into the elevator, wondering if Giorgio had misunderstood her when she'd first said she would be there for an extended stay.

She got off on the third floor, ran her key card over the lock and pushed through the door into her room.

She dropped her beach bag on the floor and stepped out of her skirt cover up before heading for the bathroom. Her bed had been made in her absence. An envelope lay on the pillow with a wrapped chocolate resting on it. The staff had been wonderful, treating her just as well as they did the Martins, even though she was the au pair.

Kinsey stripped and entered the shower. Using the shampoo provided by the hotel, she washed the salt out of her hair and off her skin, and applied a liberal amount of conditioner.

Five minutes later, she was dry. Dressed in a short black dress with a matching shawl and low heels, she strode past the empty concierge's desk. By now, Giorgio must have gone home to be with his family.

With only a few minutes to spare, Kinsey headed out of the hotel, hurrying through the winding streets to the café they'd frequented on several occasions. Though it had decent food, Kinsey didn't think the restaurant was quite up to par with the Martins' luxurious lifestyle. But they seemed to like it and were friendly with the owners.

Darkness settled around the Greek island, and lights lit many of the corners. Kinsey usually walked with the Martins to the restaurants. This trip was the first time she'd ventured out at night on her own. The children usually didn't go to sleep until after ten, and Kinsey didn't know anyone else on the island, so she hadn't been interested in exploring the nightlife.

Gathering the light shawl around her shoulders, she tucked her purse beneath her arm and stepped out smartly. She was careful not to let her heels get caught in the cobblestones as she wove through the streets and corridors between the buildings.

She hurried past the shadowy corners and alleyways, a creepy feeling spreading through her senses. Several times, she slowed her pace and glanced over her shoulder, swearing she'd heard an echoing set of footsteps. But when she paused and listened hard, she didn't hear anything but the sounds of voices from nearby homes and buildings.

Shrugging, she moved on.

Almost at the top of the terraced hillside, she heard the footsteps again. This time, they were real, and they came fast from behind her.

Kinsey stepped to the side, to allow whoever was in such a hurry to move past her on the narrow stairs. She glanced over her shoulder and waited for the owner of the footsteps to pass.

Two men in dark clothing appeared from around the corner below, wearing dark hats pulled down over their foreheads which shadowed their faces.

A trickle of fear pulsed through Kinsey. She was a lone female in a strange land. Two of them had appeared, and they were big and burly. But they appeared to be in a hurry, as if they were late for something.

They came at her, taking the steps two at a time.

Kinsey thought better of waiting for them to pass and continued her ascent, hoping to reach a better-lit area with more people around in case she ran into trouble.

But the more she climbed the twisting stairs, the closer the men came, until they almost overtook her.

She'd just decided to move aside again when she was hit in the back hard enough to send her sprawling onto her hands and knees, sliding down several steps before she stopped. "Hey, watch it!" she yelled. Her heart banging hard in her chest. *No. This can't be another mugging.*

Before she could rise to her feet and face the man who'd knocked her down, a meaty hand wrapped around her arm and yanked her to her feet. "Let go of me," she demanded and fought to break the hold on her arm.

The other man clamped a hand over her mouth, pressing a cloth over her nose with a sickly-sweet scent.

Kinsey twisted in an attempt to free herself of the man's iron grip and the cloth making it hard to breathe. But her muscles weren't cooperating, and her vision blurred. No. She couldn't pass out. She had to stay awake and find a way to escape her attackers. This outrage was not happening to her.

But it was.

As the darkness crept in around her senses, the cloth was removed. Once she could breathe fresh air, she tried to call out, but the feeble attempt at a scream came out as a pathetic murmur. "Help...me." She was lifted and thrown over the man's shoulder. Kinsey couldn't even raise her head or kick her legs.

All the self-defense training she'd taken before leaving the States did her no good when she couldn't control a single muscle. She flopped like a ragdoll as her captor ran up the steps to the main road.

2

SAM FOUND the bed and breakfast he'd reserved online, only to discover the building was a lot smaller than the pictures depicted. The view the site touted was not from the room he'd rented, but from the top of the building. Granted, it was pretty spectacular, but he'd had to climb a rickety ladder to see it.

The position high above the other surrounding structures gave him a panoramic vista of Imerovigli, the picturesque town of whitewashed buildings clinging to the hillsides overlooking the turquoise waters of the Mediterranean. Indeed, the sight was as gorgeous as the pictures on the website, but it wasn't from the comfort of his room. His suite was an interior one with no view and right off the corridor where the elderly owner, Esma Demopolis, had her apartment.

She'd been cordial and welcoming, but she could speak very little English and wanted cash up front for the entire duration of his stay on Santorini.

By the time he'd taken care of the rental business, unloaded the clothes from his duffel bag into the closet and small dresser and shoved his cellphone into his back pocket, the sun had set and darkness descended on the Greek island.

Sam's stomach rumbled. He hadn't eaten since leaving Dublin earlier that morning. Four hours, two planes and a long, stiff uphill walk later, he was famished.

He left his cave-like room, passed the landowner's door and exited the villa into a dark alley with only starlight to guide him when he wasn't in the shadows.

Sam waited at the bottom of the stairs until his vision adjusted to the limited lighting. He checked for the Ka-Bar knife he kept in a scabbard buckled around his calf. The knife had been a Christmas gift a couple years back from his Navy SEAL brother, Ronin. He'd carried it with him since. If not strapped to his leg, then packed in his checked baggage.

When he could see well enough to navigate the stone steps, he headed through the streets, back toward the coast where he'd seen several restaurants on his walk in. He wanted food and a beer. He might try the Greek liquor ouzo if the beer didn't take the edge off his temper.

His commander wouldn't be happy to know he was more wound up than ever.

His cellphone vibrated in his back pocket, making him jump and almost miss the next step. Jerking himself upright, he paused, pulled out his phone and realized it was a Facetime call from the man he'd just been thinking about. Why in hell had he paid extra on his phone plan for coverage? He didn't have an excuse to ignore all incoming calls.

He accepted the call and backed up to a little light over an entrance door in an alcove. "Colonel Cooley, sir." He found himself standing at attention—after all, his CO was in uniform.

"At ease, Magnus. You should be in Santorini by now. How was the flight?"

"I am, and great. Thanks for asking." Or rather, thanks for keeping track. His CO was not leaving his rest, relaxation and mental recuperation up to chance. "I just settled into my digs, and I'm off to find chow."

"Good. I expect a daily report of your progress."

His heart thudded against his ribs, and his fingers tightened around the cellphone. "Daily, Sir?"

"You heard me. I'm sure the wedding in Ireland was chaotic—weddings always are."

The man didn't know the half of it. And never would. Unless the event made the BBC. In which case, Sam's ass would be grounded for sure.

"You're telling me you want me to report in daily about my vacation?" Seriously? He didn't add that last word, but his tone implied it.

"Damn right. I want to know you're relaxing. Just so we're clear, your future flight status depends on it."

"Sir, I can't guarantee a specific time."

"I don't care, as long as you report in once every twenty-four hours. If I don't answer, my executive officer will."

Great. Just great. How was he supposed to relax,

knowing he was being monitored? Hell, he'd stand on his head and juggle oranges with his toes if the action kept him from being grounded. "Will do, sir."

"Good. Now, go soak up some sun. I'm planning on living vicariously through you while I'm sitting in this hell hole. Cooley out."

"Magnus out."

The call ended, leaving Sam standing in the alcove, anger pushing heat up his neck. He had half a mind to throw the device as far as he could. He'd tell the colonel he'd broken his phone and was unable make the required daily reports.

Like that would make a difference.

Colonel Cooley wouldn't let him slide one iota. He'd expect Sam to run out and buy a new phone in time to make his situation report on time.

He forced himself to loosen his hold on the phone and reached behind him to slide it into his pocket. Before he could release the device, it vibrated again.

Anger shot up like mercury dipped in hot water. He jerked the cellphone from his pocket and answered. "Seriously?" Regretting the gruff word as soon as it cleared his lips.

"Whoa, dude. Is that any way to greet your favorite brother?"

Sam pulled away the phone from his head and stared at the caller ID on the screen before letting go of the breath he'd gathered to blast his commander. "Sorry, Wyatt. I didn't know the call was from you."

Wyatt chuckled. "I certainly hope not. But I feel sorry for the schmuck you thought I was. Who was it?"

"Colonel Cooley, my CO."

"Wow, you speak to your commander like that? I'd be slapped with an Article 15 for that kind of backtalk."

"I'm glad it was you and not him. I just got off the phone with him. He wants me to report in daily." Already, Sam's thoughts had moved on to ways he could prove to the boss he was following orders. He'd have to research interesting places, beaches and historic sites he could stand in front of and take pictures of himself.

"He expects you to report in on vacation?"

"He doesn't think I know how to relax. He's hinging my flight status on my ability to calm down."

"Oh."

One word from Wyatt said a lot.

"What?" Sam couldn't believe his brother was siding with his CO. "You think I don't know how to relax, too?"

"I didn't say that, but now that you mention it…you were a little uptight at the wedding."

"And who wouldn't be? Mack and the bride's cousin were being chased by murderers." He shoved a hand through his hair. "What do you expect?"

"Hey, don't get your shorts in a twist." Wyatt paused. "So, how is the R&R going?"

"I'll let you know when I've had a chance to start it. I just got here, I'm hungry and two phone calls now are standing in the way of me and food."

"Sorry, man. I'll let you go."

Sam sighed. "I guess I am a little wound up. Was there a reason for this call? I thought you and Fiona were on your honeymoon."

"Oh, yeah, we are, but we got to thinking that lazing on the beach in Crete would be a little too much downtime. We decided to see a little more of Europe by train. I wanted to let you know we'll be there in two days."

"You do know you can't get to Santorini by train, right?"

"No? You're kidding." Wyatt laughed. "We know, but we're taking a short hop from Athens. And I think Mack and Dierdre will be flying in about the same time. I'm not sure about Ronin. Seems he's been busy in Venice. I'll see if he wants to make it another family reunion on the island."

Sam snorted. "Ireland wasn't enough?" Though his voice dripped sarcasm, he was secretly happy to be with family any chance he could get.

"What? You don't want to see your brothers again so soon?"

"You know I love you guys, but I'm sure you have much better things to do on your honeymoon than hang out with a bunch of guys." If Sam had a woman as beautiful as his brother's bride, he'd spend all his time in bed with her. No matter what continent or island they landed on.

"Oh, we're doing the whole honeymoon thing, but we're both used to a lot more activity. Relaxing is a little harder than we expected."

"Tell me about it," Sam said, his tone flat.

"Fiona and I haven't been to Santorini, and since you're already there, we thought we'd hop over and check it out."

"Actually, I'd be glad for the company, but I don't

have space in my room at the B&B for any guests." He glanced around at the white walls of the buildings around him. "I could look around for another place with space available."

"That's okay. We booked the honeymoon suite in one of the hotels in Imerovigli. We can do dinner that night. Fiona wanted to see a sunset and a sunrise on the island."

"What? No snorkeling or scuba?"

"Not this time. We have a train to catch. We'll eventually end up in Crete, as originally planned. We can dive then."

"Great. I'll see you in a couple days."

"Yeah," Wyatt said. "In the meantime, learn how to relax."

"Don't you start." Sam's hand tightened on the phone. "I have enough of a nag with my CO, I don't need the same from you."

Wyatt laughed. "Just poking the bear. You really do need to lighten up. Out here."

"Out here." Sam hit the button to end the call and pocketed the phone, a bit of a smile curling his lips. At least he wouldn't have to find entertainment for one of the fourteen days he'd be on Santorini. Having his brothers here would cut some of the boredom.

His belly grumbled, reminding him he was on his way to the restaurants he knew he'd find eventually.

He'd almost reached the top of the hill when he saw a couple of big, shadowy figures ahead of him, heading the same direction...toward the main road that crossed the island. One of them seemed to be carrying a large package or sack full of something.

The hairs on the back of Sam's neck stood at attention when he realized the something being carried had long blond hair hanging down, swaying with each step.

Within a second, he recognized the package was a woman and she appeared to be unconscious.

Alarm bells went off in Sam's head, and his body tensed. He didn't know the story, but the way the man was handling the woman couldn't be right. And the men were dressed in dark clothing and dark hats.

Fuck. They had either killed the woman or knocked her unconscious and were kidnapping her.

Sam only hesitated a moment. He didn't want to get involved in drama when he was under orders to relax, but he couldn't ignore the situation unfolding in front of him.

From his vantage point, he could see another path that led to the same outlet the two men would ultimately come to. If he took that path, he might arrive at that point at the same time.

Without thinking about what he'd do when he confronted the assailants, he raced through a narrow corridor between buildings at breakneck speed, arriving at what he hoped was the intersection where he'd run into them.

When he got there, he didn't find the two men and the woman they were carrying. For a moment, he thought he might have taken a wrong turn, or the men might have ducked into a building. No sooner had the thoughts crossed his mind than he heard footsteps and muttered, angry words spoken in a foreign language that didn't sound like Greek. It sounded more like Russian. A moment later, his quarry appeared around the corner of a building, the empty-handed one in the lead.

Sam didn't know if they were armed, but he wasn't taking any chances. He pulled his Ka-Bar knife out of the sheath on his calf and waited in the shadows.

As the first man came abreast of him, he jumped out, grabbed him from behind and yanked him back against his chest, pressing his knife to the man's throat. "Drop the woman," Sam said in his most threatening tone.

The man carrying the woman froze.

"Drop her," Sam demanded.

The man shrugged the limp woman off his shoulder and let her drop to the hard stone steps. She lay as still as death.

Then all hell broke loose.

With his hands freed of his captive, the big guy launched himself at Sam.

Sam shifted the guy he held at knife-point to take the brunt of the big man's hit. The force of the impact sent both Sam and his prisoner backward.

Sam's back hit a wall with enough force to knock the air from his chest. He fought to fill his lungs, the weight of the man in front of him pressing against him.

Then the man he'd been holding cocked his elbow and jammed it into Sam's gut.

Sam's grip loosened.

Now completely out of breath and pain shooting though his belly, Sam went into survival mode. He swung hard, his knife catching the man's sleeve, tearing into the fabric and slicing his arm.

The man spun and swung, landing a punch against Sam's jaw.

More pain bolted through him, making him angry and ready for the confrontation to end. Having grown up with three brothers, Sam was used to fighting, wrestling and punching. Growing up he could get out of just about any situation his brothers put him in. His Army survival and fighting skills only added to his abilities.

Sam slammed his palm into the lead guy's nose and felt the cartilage crunch.

The man yelped and clapped his hand to his face, leaving open his belly for the punch Sam hit him with next. He doubled over and Sam brought up his knee, slamming the guy again in the face.

He went down and lay still, clearing the path for his buddy.

The big guy had weight and bulk on his side, but he was slow. He rushed at Sam.

Sam stepped to the right.

Too late to alter his direction, the big guy plowed head-first into the side of the building like a character in a silent movie.

With just a gentle shove, Sam sent him toppling back down the stairs he'd come up carrying the female.

Before either man could regain consciousness, Sam lifted the woman in his arms and ran back down the stairs, took the first left turn and kept moving until he was sure he'd put enough distance between him and the men who'd captured the woman. When he felt certain he was safely away from danger, he laid the woman on the ground and checked to verify whether she was alive or dead.

At the faint flutter of a pulse, he sucked in a deep breath and let it out slowly. If the woman were dead, and he'd been caught carrying her, how would he have explained to the police that he wasn't the murderer? Not only would he be stuck with a murder rap, he was on foreign soil, a member of the US military and in possession of a deadly knife. "Hey, lady," he whispered, tapping his hand against her cheek. "Wake up."

She lay still, not responding.

He lowered his head against her chest and listened. She was breathing normally and her heartbeat was strong. They must have drugged her.

If he was smart, he'd take her to the nearest hospital and dump her ass. Again, how would he explain how he'd come into possession of an unconscious woman? She might awaken and accuse him of the kidnapping, or even rape.

Hell, what was he supposed to do with her?

With no other option apparent, he lifted her into his arms, carried her back down the many steps to the B&B and tiptoed past the landlady's room. Mrs. Demopolis would have a conniption fit if she saw him carrying an unconscious woman into a room she'd rented him. She might call the cops and have him hauled off to a jail where he didn't speak the language and couldn't talk his way out of prosecution.

As long as the woman didn't seem to be in any physical distress, he'd keep her in his room until she woke and could tell him where she was staying. Then he'd make sure he got her there safely and leave her to fend for herself.

With that plan in mind, he juggled the woman in his arms, reaching into his pocket for the ancient key to his room.

He'd just pushed his door open when another set of hinges creaked loudly. Sam, clutching the unconscious woman to his chest, dove into the room and kicked the door shut behind him. He ran through the sitting area and deposited his burden on the bed, piling up the pillows on one side of her body to hide her from view. If he wasn't mistaken, the landlady would be knocking in five...four...three...

Knock, knock, knock.

The soft rapping made Sam's heart stop and then hammer against his ribs. He rolled over the woman, covering her in the blanket and made it appear as if the bed was in disarray, not filled with a body.

Another knock sounded.

"Coming," he called out. He rushed into the bathroom, ran water over his hands and came out carrying the hand towel as if he'd been washing up when he heard the knocking.

Mrs. Demopolis stood in the doorway, a frown pulling her thick, white eyebrows together in a V. "Did you find a restaurant in which to eat?" she asked in her broken English.

"Uh. No. I didn't."

"Your room is okay?" She leaned to the side, attempting to peer around him.

"My room is fine, thank you," he said, shifting enough to keep her view of the bed blocked.

"You're hungry. Do you like gyros?"

His stomach groaned loudly, or he would have lied and said he wasn't hungry.

Mrs. D smiled. "Maybe moussaka?"

Her friendly smile threw him off. Before she'd been all business. Now she wanted to be friendly? "I don't know. I've never had it."

"I'll bring some."

He raised his hands. "Oh, no. Thank you. That's not necessary. I understood this place to only serve breakfast."

"I made extra. It's no problem." She left before he could protest further.

On the one hand, he was glad she'd left. On the other, he knew she'd be back, and he couldn't let her find the woman in the bed.

Quickly, he threw the pillows into the bathtub and then carried the woman into the ensuite and laid her on them.

Right as Sam pulled the curtain around the bathtub, the landlady sailed into his little apartment carrying a tray filled with a casserole, two plates, a green salad, a teapot and cups.

"I eat with you. No?" She smiled at him. "Plenty food."

He couldn't say no, not without offending the older woman.

As she set the tray on the little table in the middle of the room, liquid splashed out of the teapot.

"I clean." She hurried toward the bathroom.

Damn, damn, damn.

Sam hurried after her, but he wasn't quick enough to head her off before she made it to the bathroom. For an older woman, she was fast.

The little Greek woman swept in, grabbed a washcloth off the counter, wet it in the sink and started back toward the sitting area.

A soft moan sounded from the bathtub.

Sam's heart pounded, and he made a matching moaning sound to cover the first one. For good measure, he patted his stomach. "Your moussaka smells good enough to eat." He smiled, took the woman's arm and led her back into the main room, shutting the bathroom door behind her.

Once he had her seated at the little table, he didn't wait for her to serve the food. Instead, he cut out a small portion from the casserole dish and slid it onto one of the empty plates. He set that plate in front of Mrs. D. "Don't wait on me. Eat," he encouraged.

The woman gave him a weak smile and looked around with a frown, as if she wasn't sure what to do if she wasn't doing the serving.

Sam slapped a scoop of the Greek dish on his plate, grabbed his fork and dug in, his ears pricked for noise from the bathroom

This nightmare of a vacation couldn't get worse, could it? He hated to ask what next. Instead, he sat on the edge of his seat, waiting for the woman in the bathtub to scream and bring down the wrath of Mrs. D and the Santorini police department on his head.

By the time he'd choked down the moussaka, which actually melted in his mouth in a delightful explosion of flavors, and downed a cup of strong tea, his nerves were stretched so thin he thought he might snap before Mrs. D left the room.

The landlady motioned toward the casserole dish. "I will leave some with you in case you are hungry later."

"The food was excellent. Thank you," he said and meant it. He'd been hungry earlier, but the stress of worrying about the woman in the bathtub and Mrs. Demopolis discovering her killed the majority of his appetite.

Mrs. D scooped a portion onto a plate, covered it with a cloth napkin and set it on the table. "Thank you for allowing me to share my food with you."

"No, ma'am. I should be thanking you."

She patted his cheek. "Such a handsome man. Wish that I were thirty years younger..." She laughed and carried the tray out of the room. "*Kalinychta*," she said. "Goodnight."

Sam shut the door and leaned his forehead against the wood paneling, listening for the sound of Mrs. D's disappearing footsteps and the soft click of her door closing.

Immediately, he carried a chair to the door and shoved it beneath the doorknob.

Only then did he run for the bathroom, throw open the door and fling back the curtain.

The bathtub was empty.

3

KINSEY STRUGGLED UPWARD as if swimming from the bottom of the deepest, darkest ocean to the surface. When she finally found the energy to lift her eyelids she stared up, not at sunlight but the soft glow of a light fixture overhead.

She glanced around, her arms touching a cool, smooth surface, her body lying on something soft. A curtain surrounded her on one side and white tile on the other three. Unable grasp the significance, she stared up at a curious, shiny fixture. A showerhead?

She was lying in a bathtub, her body barely functioning and her limbs lead weights. What the hell had happened? Then, as slowly as she'd come to understand she was in a bathtub, she remembered the two men on the stairs between the buildings and the fight she'd put up until one had pressed a rag to her mouth and nose.

They drugged me.

Her pulse raced, but she couldn't react as fast as she

wanted. The soft hum of voices sounded from somewhere nearby. Were her captors in the other room, waiting to perform whatever dastardly deed they had planned?

Kinsey made a mental evaluation of her physical condition. She still wore the same dress she'd had on earlier. The garment wasn't torn or soiled. Her shoes were gone, but that could have happened in the scuffle. As far as she could tell, she hadn't been undressed or raped. But that didn't guarantee the dreaded act wouldn't happen if she didn't get herself up and out of the bathtub and whatever building they held her in.

Slowly, her ability to govern her own movement returned and she could wiggle her toes. Then her fingers, and finally lift her arms and legs. She pushed to a sitting position and listened.

She could make out the sound of a woman's voice and that of a man. If she called out, would the woman come to her rescue, or was the female part of this abduction?

Kinsey yanked back the curtain, gripped the side of the bathtub and pulled herself out, slumping onto the floor. She lay for a moment, her face pressed to the smooth tile, willing her muscles to respond.

From the sounds outside the door, someone was leaving. If she wanted to get out of there, she'd have to make a move.

She pushed to her hands and knees, her head spinning and her stomach churning. When the room quit revolving, she crawled to the sink, reached up, grabbed the edge of the counter and pulled herself up to stand.

The gray fog swept in around her vision, threatening to send her back to the black abyss. Kinsey blinked several times and focused on the shiny faucet. *Don't pass out!*

She searched the immediate vicinity for anything she could use as a weapon, her gaze landing on a brand new bar of soap. It wasn't much, but it was all she could get her hands on in a hurry. She quickly closed the shower curtain, grabbed the bar and slid into the corner behind the door as footsteps sounded, moving in her direction.

Kinsey dragged in deep breaths, her heart racing, her legs barely steady enough to hold her upright.

The door swung open, almost slamming into her before she stopped it with one hand.

A man appeared in front of her, swept aside the shower curtain and stared down at the bathtub where she'd been lying moments before.

Now was her moment. If she could hit him hard enough, she might knock him out and have enough time to make a run for it.

She swung her arm as hard as she could, which wasn't much, considering she could barely stand. The soap bar connected with the man's temple.

He staggered forward, grabbing air in a desperate attempt to latch onto something to break his fall. His fingers tangled into the shower curtain, and he tumbled into the bathtub, landing on the pillows.

Kinsey pushed away from the wall and staggered out of the bathroom into a room with a queen-sized bed, a small table and an armchair. Her gaze darted left and right, looking for the second man of the two who'd accosted her in the alley.

The room was empty but for the man she'd clobbered in the bathtub.

Her momentum carried her clumsily toward the door. She reached for the knob, but a hand clamped down over her mouth and an arm wrapped around her body, trapping her own arms to her sides. He wasn't as burly as the first guy who'd grabbed her. This man was lean and muscular, but too strong for Kinsey to break free of.

She tried to scream, the only sound coming out as a pathetic hum that wouldn't be heard past the wooden panel of the door.

"Don't scream, and I'll let you go."

A deep, resonant voice said against her ear.

"I promise. I'm not going to hurt you."

Kinsey froze, bunching her muscles in case she got another chance to make a run for it.

"Do you promise not to scream?" he asked.

His breath brushed warm on her neck. She nodded, gathering a deep breath to prepare for the mother of all screams.

"And don't rush out of the room. The landlady will kick me out, and I don't relish the idea of finding another place to stay this late at night. Promise you won't run out of here and make a lot of noise?"

Again, she didn't have much of a choice. She nodded and waited, her pulse pounding so loud against her eardrums she could barely hear herself think.

Then he released her mouth, dropped his arms from around her and stepped away.

Her pulse leaped and Kinsey grabbed for the doorknob.

"Please. Just be quiet when you leave," he whispered.

Anger blasted through Kinsey. She might be gullible for believing he would release her so easily, but she wouldn't let the bastard get away with scaring the crap out of her without getting a piece of her mind. She spun and faced the antagonist. "Why the hell did you drug me, if you're just letting me go anyway?"

The man took another step backward and held up both hands. "Look, lady, I wasn't the one who drugged you, or was making off with you into the night. I just happened by and stopped the two guys who had you from taking you to who knows where."

Kinsey frowned. He sounded American and he was really handsome, but that didn't make him trustworthy or her friend. "Why should I believe you?"

He laughed. "Don't believe me. But, please, leave. I've had enough drama for one day."

She turned and placed her hand on the doorknob again. "You're not stopping me?"

"No." He waved at the small room. "I didn't want to bring you here in the first place."

"Then why did you?" she asked, her back to him, her body braced and ready to yank open the door and run, if he attacked.

"I couldn't leave you lying on the steps. Those goons might have come back and collected you after I left. I didn't get this bruised cheek just to let them pick up where they left off."

She glanced over her shoulder and studied him. Though she didn't want to trust him, his words and voice sounded sincere.

He touched a hand to the side of his face where a purple smudge was just beginning to show.

The man had hair the color of glossy coal and eyes as blue as the Mediterranean Sea. He was ruggedly handsome, with the shadow of a beard darkening his chin. "They hit you?"

He shrugged. "One of them got in a couple of punches, but I left them both hurting."

"Why would they attack me?"

The man rolled his eyes. "Really? A lone female walking around at night? Are you that dumb?"

Kinsey glared at the man. She felt stupid for going out at night alone, but this man had no right to call her dumb. "I was late to meet my employers at a restaurant." Her eyes widened. "What time is it?"

"After ten thirty."

"I was supposed to be there at eight. I was out for that long?" She wondered if the Martins were looking for her.

"Yeah. The landlady invited herself to share her dinner with me while you were sleeping it off in the bathroom."

"In the bathtub. What's with that? Why did you ditch me in a tub?"

He snorted. "How was I supposed to explain an

unconscious woman in my bed to the lady renting me this room?"

Kinsey crossed her arms over her chest and narrowed her eyes. "Why didn't you take me to a hospital?"

He shook his head and planted his hands on his hips. "Again, how was I supposed to explain to the authorities why I was carrying around an unconscious woman?"

She flung her hands in the air. "I could have been dying, and you refused to take me to seek medical attention?"

"Calm down. You weren't in any physical distress. I checked for a pulse. You were breathing fine. I figured those men must have drugged you."

Kinsey pressed a hand to her mouth and her stomach roiled. "They shoved a sweet-smelling cloth in my face, and I blacked out."

"There you go. You were unconscious. I fought them off and then I was stuck with you until you came to." He walked toward her.

Kinsey gasped and shrank against the door. "What are you doing?"

"I'm opening the door so you can leave. I didn't want you here in the first place."

Her back stiffened. "Well, you don't have to be so rude about it. I didn't ask to be abducted."

"Then we agree, the sooner you and I part, the better." He paused with his hand on the doorknob. "Just keep it quiet leaving. I don't want Mrs. Demopolis to get the idea I have a woman in my room."

"Do you do that often?" Kinsey asked, lowering her voice.

"I got here today. Since then, I've barely had two minutes to myself."

"Let me remedy the situation." She raised her eyebrows. "If you'll open the door, and tell me exactly where I am, I'll be on my way." She tried to sound confident, even though she had no idea which side of the island she was on. Or if she was even on the same island.

He nodded toward her feet. "Are you okay with going back to your room barefoot?"

"I'll be fine. Most of the steps around here are stone. I haven't seen too much gravel."

"Then by all means…" The man opened the door and waved an arm toward the corridor. "*Hasta la vista.*"

Shaking her head, she rolled her eyes. "You're in Greece, not Spain or Mexico."

"Since we're both American, does it matter?"

She laughed. "Not really." Kinsey touched a finger to her temple in a mock salute. "Thank you for rescuing me." But she didn't step out of the door. Her feet wouldn't budge from where they were on the room side of the threshold.

Her knees wobbled then her entire body shook.

"The door's open," the man said and waved her toward the exit again.

"I know. I'm going." She tried to lift her foot, but she couldn't. The thought of stepping out into the night paralyzed her. "I'm sorry. I don't know what's wrong with me," she whispered. "You haven't told me where I am, and…I can't seem to move past the door."

The man drew in a deep breath and let it out. "I guess I can't blame you. After being attacked in the dark, I'd be afraid of venturing out on my own. Come on." He hooked her elbow in his hand. "I'll walk you back to wherever you're staying."

This time, her feet left the floor and she was able to step over the threshold into the corridor on the other side.

Her rescuer pressed a finger to his lips, tiptoed past the next door down the hallway and pushed through another door to the outside.

Once out in the open, Kinsey glanced around, her stomach knotting. She didn't recognize any of the buildings. But then, they were tightly packed against the hillside and all looked the same in the darkness—white with blue-tiled roofs.

"I don't know why I should trust you," she said as she walked alongside him. "I don't even know your name. All I know is that you're American. But I've met a lot of American men I wouldn't trust with my best friend, or worst enemy."

He laughed. "My name is Sam. You have no reason to trust me, other than I saved you from two men who seemed bent on taking you somewhere against your will."

Kinsey stumbled on the next step. She was glad Sam still had his hand on her elbow to steady her. Her legs weren't quite as trustworthy as she needed them to be on the hills. "I wonder where they were taking me?"

Sam's grip on her arm tightened. "I don't know."

"And I don't want to find out." She glanced up at him. "By the way, my name is Kinsey Phillips."

She shivered in the cool night air, realizing for the first time that she'd lost her light shawl in her fight with the two men. "I'm not sure where we are."

"Do you remember the name of your hotel?"

"Porto Takisi."

"I passed that coming in today. It shouldn't be too hard to find."

"Easy for you to say. You arrived here with your eyes open." When she thought about it, the evening could have ended on a much worse note.

"You have a point. You're in luck. I'm pretty good at land navigation."

She glanced sideways. He carried himself with the pride and bearing of someone who'd known military service. "Were you in the Army?"

He smiled. "Why do you ask?"

She shrugged then focused on the path ahead and avoiding small pebbles. "Just the way you talk and the way you carry yourself."

He didn't say anything for a few more steps. "Yes, I was in the Army."

She nodded. "Infantry?"

"Aviation."

A pebble dug into the tender area of her instep, and she dipped low, taking the weight off that foot.

"Find a rock?" he asked.

"Yes, a little one." She straightened and forced a smile to her lips. "I'm fine."

"Like hell, you are."

Before she could utter a protest, Sam lifted her into his arms.

"You can't carry me all the way to my hotel. That's just crazy." She slung an arm around his neck to ease the burden on his arms. She would never admit it aloud, but she liked that he lifted her so easily. And his hard body felt good against her softer one. Her attraction to him shocked her. "Put me down."

"I will," he said, but belied his words by continuing along his way. "When we get there."

"You'll hurt your back."

"Will you talk my ear off?"

"Maybe," she said, holding her dress close to her thigh. "If you don't let me walk on my own two feet."

"Fine. Have it your way." He set her on her feet. "We're here." He turned her around and pointed toward the hotel.

Thankful to see the familiar building, Kinsey hurried forward and then stopped, remembering the man who'd been key in her ability to return to her hotel. "Thank you for saving my life and making sure I made it back to my hotel safely. I don't know how I can repay you."

"Forget about it. Just don't run around the streets at night alone."

She stood at attention and saluted him. "I won't." Now that she was back on familiar territory, she didn't need him anymore. But she was hesitant to walk away. "I'm sure you need to head back to your room. Thank you again."

He stood straight, unbending. "If you don't mind, I'd

like to see you to your door. I've come this far, I might as well make certain you make it the rest of the way."

"You don't have to," she said. "I've been at this hotel for a week with no problems."

"Other than nearly being kidnapped."

"I wasn't at the hotel when that happened," she argued.

He shrugged. "Still, I feel like it's my duty."

Kinsey bristled. "You're not responsible for me, or anything. I really can manage on my own." She sighed and nodded. "I know. I know. Barring thugs in the streets at night."

"I'm already here. Humor me." When she still hesitated, he touched her arm. "If I wanted to harm you, I would have done it before you were conscious so that you wouldn't talk my ear off. I won't hurt you. I just want to see you to your door. If you want the concierge to come along as a chaperone, I'm all for it."

Not wanting to appear churlish, and feeling a little foolish, Kinsey pressed her lips together in a tight smile. "Fine. You can walk me to my room." She was halfway across the lobby before he stopped her with a touch on her elbow.

"Do you have a key tucked into your bra or something?"

"What kind of question is that?" Then she realized he had a point. "Damn. You're right, and I forgot. When they attacked me, I must have dropped my purse." Mrs. Martin gave her one of her old purses when she'd hired on with the family. Now it was as gone as the purse she'd had stolen in Athens. Her chest tightened. She couldn't catch a break, lately. But, she refused to dwell on what she couldn't change. Instead, she marched to the desk and asked for a replacement key for her room number.

The clerk, a dark-haired woman she hadn't met, glanced down at the computer screen and tapped keys. "Kinsey Phillips, you say?" she asked.

"Yes. I've been here for the past week with the Martins as their au pair."

The woman's fingers flew over the keys, a frown denting her smooth brow. "Are you sure you're at the right hotel, miss?"

"This is the Porto Takisi?" Kinsey looked left and then right. She recognized the lobby as the same décor she'd been walking past all week.

"Yes, this is the Porto Takisi," the clerk said. "But I have no record of a Kinsey Phillips staying here now or for the past seven days."

Kinsey's stomach clenched. "What do you mean?" Kinsey leaned over the counter and tried to see what was on the screen in front of the woman.

"I'm sorry, miss, but I don't have you as a guest here."

"What about the Martins? I'm in the connecting room to theirs on the third floor."

"The Martins checked out this morning at ten o'clock. They only reserved the one room."

"And I had the connecting room." Kinsey's voice rose. "Go see for yourself. My clothes, everything I own, is in that room."

"I'm sorry miss, but registered guests are in the

room the Martins occupied and in the rooms on either side."

She planted her hands on the counter, anger and panic building in her chest. "Then what the hell did you do with my clothes and suitcase?"

The clerk looked around nervously. "Miss, if you would like to step into our conference room, I'll have a manager come speak with you."

"Damn right, you'll get the manager." Kinsey pinched the bridge of her nose and turned toward the conference room. "This situation cannot be happening, again."

Sam slipped an arm around her waist and walked with her. "What do you mean, again?"

She leaned into the strength of his body, thankful he had insisted on staying with her. "I was mugged in Athens. The bastard stole my purse with every cent I own. I didn't have a passport, money, credit cards, or anything. All I had was my suitcase with the few clothes I brought with me." She flung her arm out to the side. "And now they're telling me I don't even have those?"

"Just wait and hear what the manager has to say." He led her into the room and pulled out a chair, urging her to sit. "This has to be a misunderstanding."

"It better be. I'm still waiting for my replacement passport from the U.S. Embassy in Athens." She tipped back her head, remembering Giorgio's words of earlier that evening. He'd asked if she'd be leaving soon, as well. Bile rose up her throat. She swallowed hard. "Holy hell, what did the clerk mean by the Martins checked out this morning? I work for them. They owe me a week's pay. How the hell am I supposed to live without money?" She was halfway out of the chair when a man wearing a dark suit with Milonas printed on the name tag pinned to his lapel entered the room.

"Miss Phillips?" the manager said.

Again, this man was not one Kinsey recognized. "Where is Mr. Petras, the regular manager?"

"Miss, I'm Alexia Milonas, the manager. I've been here all week. And we do not have a Mr. Petras working here."

"What?" Kinsey's head spun. "I spoke to him several times. Maybe he wasn't the manager, but he worked here. I've never seen you before now."

Milonas stood with his hands clasped together. "And I don't recall seeing you. I take pride in introducing myself to all of the hotel's guests."

"Then you will have met my employers, Lois and Timothy Martin and their children."

He nodded. "I had the pleasure of meeting them and wished them a safe journey today as they checked out of their room."

She leaned forward, her pulse quickening. "Then you would know they had another room reserved beside theirs. The one adjoining their room. The one on the left when you're facing their door."

"Miss, that room has been reserved by a man from Istanbul for the past week."

Her heart sank into the pit of her belly, and her head spun. She assumed her reaction had a little to do with whatever the thugs had used to knock her out, but she couldn't still be so strung out that she misunderstood what had occurred over the past seven days. "I stayed in that room for the past week. My things are in that room. Take me up there, and I'll show you."

Milonas shook his head, his lips thinning. "Miss, I can't do that. There are guests in that room."

She pounded her fist on the counter. "You take me up there now, or I'll go to the third floor by myself. My belongings are in that room."

The manager's eyes narrowed. "I'll take you, but I ask that you don't cause a disturbance with the guests now occupying the room."

Kinsey drew in a breath and let it out slowly, trying to keep calm when her world was crashing all around her. Again. "Just take me."

4

SAM WASN'T sure what was going on, but the woman he'd saved was proving to be even more drama than he'd originally anticipated. But she didn't appear to be lying, nor did she seem to have anyone in her corner. As much as he knew he should for his own welfare, he couldn't walk away and leave her stranded and alone in a foreign country with no money or identification documents.

Milonas glanced across Kinsey's shoulder to Sam. "I'll take Miss Phillips up to the room."

Sam gave the manager a level stare. "If she's going, I'm accompanying her."

The manager raised his brow and turned to Kinsey. "And he is...?"

She bit down on her bottom lip and then blurted out, "My fiancé."

How Sam maintained a poker face through her

announcement, he wasn't sure, but he did. What in hell made Kinsey say he was her fiancé?

Since Milonas seemed to accept the explanation, Sam didn't bother to enlighten him with the truth. He followed Kinsey and the hotel manager out of the conference room to the elevator. On the third floor, they stepped out and walked to a room halfway down a long hallway.

"Please, let me handle the guest," the manager said.

Kinsey's eyes narrowed, but she nodded.

The manager raised his hand and knocked lightly on the door.

For a long moment, no one responded.

"You see? No one is in that room because it was assigned to me," Kinsey said, with a wave toward the door. "Use your master key. My suitcase is in there."

Instead, Milonas raised his hand and knocked again.

Kinsey waited, tapping her bare toes on the carpet. "Just use your master key," she muttered. "I don't understand why you're wasting your time knocking."

As the last word left her mouth, the door opened, and a man wearing a fluffy white bathrobe peered out and spoke in Greek.

Milonas responded, pointed to Kinsey and made another statement.

"What are you saying?" Kinsey asked.

"I'm apologizing for disturbing this man's stay and explaining that you think this is your room and that you left personal items here. He has graciously invited you to look around inside for your things." Milonas smiled and nodded. "Make your search quick."

The man in the robe stepped back and opened the door wider, allowing Kinsey, Milonas and Sam to enter.

Kinsey ran to the closet, flung open the door and gasped. "Where are my clothes? My shoes? Everything?"

"I told you, Mr. Vidales has been here all week. You will not find your belongings in this room." Milonas motioned toward the door. "Now, I insist you leave and allow my guest to retire for the night. The hour is quite late."

"No way." Kinsey crossed her arms over her chest. "I don't know what you're pulling or why the Martins left without telling me, but you're not getting away with stealing my stuff."

"Please, step out into the hallway, Miss Phillips." Milonas attempted to take Kinsey's arm and physically force her out of the room.

Sam's hackles rose, and he stepped between Kinsey and the manager, his jaw hardening. He'd stood back while Kinsey searched the room, but he wouldn't stand for the manager pushing her around. "Let go of Miss Phillips." Sam used a low dangerous tone.

The manager maintained his grip for another full second.

"Now," Sam insisted.

Milonas released Kinsey's arm. "Please take your fiancée out of the hotel before I have security escort her off the premises. And if I find her anywhere near the Porto Takisi again, I will alert the local authorities and have her arrested for trespass."

"You can't do this to me," Kinsey whispered. "That

suitcase held all I own. Do you have a lost and found department?"

"I'm sorry, miss, we do not."

"Look, I don't give a damn about your room. But without my suitcase, I have nothing. Do you hear me? Nothing." Tears welled in her eyes and slipped down her cheeks.

Sam touched her cheek and then wrapped an arm around her waist and led her out into the hallway.

Milonas spoke to the man in the room and closed the door between them. He marched to the elevator, punched the button and waited for the doors to slide open.

Sam had the urge to plant his fist in the prick's face. What man could treat a woman so callously? Then again, what if she'd suffered a brain trauma in her altercation with the thugs in the street?

Any way he looked at it, Sam couldn't abandon Kinsey. She had no one to turn to and nothing to live on until she found her suitcase. Even with her suitcase, she had no money and no identification. She could be a con artist, for all he knew. He glanced at her, startled at the thought. Could his character judgment be that far off?

He shook his head.

No. She might be confused, but she wasn't conning him.

The fact was, he couldn't leave her to fend for herself. Not in the middle of the night. Not on a beautiful Greek island that had proven so inhospitable.

The elevator lowered them to the lobby where Sam ushered Kinsey across the smooth marble floor.

She perked up when she spotted the concierge's desk. "What about Giorgio, the concierge? He knows me. We talked every day."

Milonas frowned. "Our concierge's name is Nicolas Roussos. We don't have a Giorgio working at the Porto Takisi."

"Oh, come on." She waved a hand. "You can't tell me everyone I came into contact with at the hotel no longer works here." Kinsey turned to Sam. "Just how long was I unconscious? A year?"

"An hour, tops," he replied. "Look, we're not getting anywhere with these people. Let's come back in the morning when the day shift is on duty."

Kinsey glared at Milonas. "I'll be back. I want my suitcase, and I'm not giving up until I find it."

Milonas stared past her to Sam. "I suggest you seek medical attention for your fiancée, sir. And keep her away from this hotel and our guests."

"Why, you—" Kinsey took a step toward Milonas, her hands bunching into fists.

Sam caught her arm and pulled her tightly against his side. "We're leaving. But we will return to get to the bottom of this." With Kinsey pinned to his side, he left the hotel.

"I don't know what they're pulling, but I stayed an entire week in that hotel. I worked for the Martins and 327 was my room." She wrapped her arms around her middle. "I'm not hallucinating. I'm thinking clearly."

The ferocity of her tone and the way she held her body so tense couldn't be an act. The woman was telling the truth and was adamant about it.

48

"No matter what, it's late, I'm tired, and you need to sleep off whatever those goons drugged you with."

She stopped walking and stood as still as a statue. "You don't believe me, do you?"

Sam scrubbed a hand through his hair. "I don't know what to believe. I saved you from kidnapping, you were unconscious for a while and then you insisted you stayed at a hotel, in a room someone else is occupying. If you were me, what would you think?"

Kinsey opened her mouth, closed it and sighed, her shoulders slumping. "I wouldn't believe me, either." She sank onto the steps at the front of the hotel. "I came to Greece for a new start, and my experience has been nothing but hell since I got here."

"Tell me about it." Sam dropped down beside her. "So, let me help you."

"I can't keep taking advantage of you. You've done so much for me already."

"What choice do you have?"

She didn't want to accept his generosity, indicating her self-determining spirit.

That spark of independence made him admire her more. "I could go to the American Embassy and see if they can get me back to the States."

"The embassy is in Athens. Plus, you don't have a place to stay the night."

"I can sleep on the beach," she said then sighed.

"What if the two dudes who tried to make off with you once find you on the beach? Who's to stop them this time?" Sam reasoned.

Kinsey wrapped her arms around her legs. "I don't

have anything but this stupid dress. They took my suitcase, my clothes and the only photographs I had of my family." She sniffed. "They were all I had left."

"You can take more photos when you get back Stateside."

She rested her chin on her knees. "No, I can't. They're dead. My parents died in a car crash last winter."

Sam's chest tightened. He couldn't imagine the anguish of losing any member of his close-knit family. "What about siblings? Don't you have any brothers and sisters?"

A big tear rolled down her cheek. "No."

"Friends?"

She shook her head again. "No."

"Not even one?"

Her lips twisted. "My ex-boyfriend cut me off from what few friends I kept in touch with after leaving school. And I worked for an elderly man and didn't have any other co-workers to talk socialize with." Another giant tear rolled down her face. With a quick swipe, she rubbed away the tears. "Look, you've done enough. I'll be all right." She straightened and wiped the tears from her face. "I always land on my feet."

He pointed to her toes. "You aren't wearing shoes."

She laughed. "Doesn't matter. Barefoot, wearing heels or tennis shoes, I'll be okay." Kinsey stood, squared her shoulders, stepped out onto a pebble and stumbled.

Sam shot to his feet. Muttering a curse beneath his

breath, he scooped her into his arms and carried her back the way they'd come.

"What are you doing?" She looped her arm around his shoulder. "You can't keep saving me. I have to survive on my own."

"Yeah, well you can start doing that tomorrow. I know I won't sleep worth a damn if you're out wandering the streets, barefooted."

"Where do you propose I should stay the night? And don't say in your room." Her body stiffened. "I don't know you that well."

"Let me introduce myself properly," he said without slowing his pace. "I'm Samuel Magnus. I'm a US Army Black Hawk helicopter pilot. I have a top-secret clearance, and America has enough faith in me to allow me to ferry the best of the best into the worst situations. What's not to trust?" He continued. "And if that's not good enough, I promise that if I did anything stupid, my three brothers would kick my ass from here to tomorrow."

Kinsey laughed, the sound ending on a choking sob. "Well, at least you have brothers."

"For tonight, I'll induct you as an honorary member of my crazy, dysfunctional family. Tomorrow, you can sort out things for yourself."

Kinsey relaxed against him. "Have you always been a knight in shining armor?"

"Far from it, according to my commander."

"What?" She laughed. "Don't tell me you're the black sheep?"

"Kind of. I'm supposed to be on vacation to learn how to relax, unwind and quit taking so many risks."

Kinsey leaned back and stared into his eyes. "Really?" She shook her head. "I'm sorry to be the reason for you failing so miserably."

"You didn't ask to be abducted or drugged."

"And you didn't ask to be my rescuer. I promise to get out of your hair tomorrow. As soon as I reclaim my suitcase and arrange a ride back to the mainland."

"How will you do that if you have no money?"

"I'll figure out something. The main thing is that I'm not your responsibility. You're here on vacation, not on a mission to babysit a sad sack like me."

Though she sounded optimistic, the confidence didn't quite come through in her voice. Sam's chest tightened. Tomorrow, he'd help her sort out things. He wouldn't rest until he knew she would be all right. So much for relaxing on the island paradise of Santorini.

They'd arrived back at the B&B.

"Sneaking me by your landlady would be easier if I'm walking on my own," Kinsey whispered.

Sam opened the exterior door and set her on her feet. Tomorrow, he'd buy her a pair of shoes and something besides that dress to wear. She couldn't go around in the warm island sunshine in a cocktail dress.

One fact was crystal clear. With Kinsey around, he wouldn't be bored. But what would he report to his commander the following day? He sure as hell wasn't telling him that he'd gotten into a fight over a woman and invited this virtual stranger to share his room. Especially since he couldn't be certain she wasn't delusional or hallucinating about a suitcase, a room in a hotel and working for some people named Martin.

They successfully navigated the hallway and entered his room without being stopped by the ever-present Mrs. Demopolis.

Sam figured she had finally gone to bed, now that the time was well past midnight.

One night down on his two-week vacation. The hours had been anything but tedious and had zoomed by rather than dragging.

Kinsey stood in the middle of the room in her rumpled black dress and her bare feet. Her long, honey-blond hair lay in wild disarray around her shoulders. For the first time since he'd met her, Sam got a really good look at the woman.

She was medium height, slim, athletic and pretty. Her hair fell down the middle of her back in long, loose waves. And her eyes were as blue as a Texas summer sky.

His groin tightened. Hell, he didn't need the complication of being attracted to his little refugee.

Kinsey pointed to the overstuffed armchair in one corner of the room. "I can sleep in that chair."

"Good, because there's no way I could." He'd slept in some pretty crappy positions before. But sleeping in the armchair would guarantee a sleepless night. His tall frame couldn't begin to curl up in that tight of a space.

She smiled. "I admit, the bathtub wasn't all that bad with the pillows lining the bottom." She laughed. "Though waking up to tile walls and a shower curtain was a bit disconcerting."

"Sorry. I had to put you somewhere out of sight of my nosy, but kind, landlady." He retrieved the pillows from the bathroom, tossing one on the chair and the other on the bed. "You're welcome to go first in the bathroom."

"Thank you." She stopped in the doorway and tilted her head. "I don't suppose you have a spare T-shirt I could borrow? The dress is pretty, but not that comfortable, especially for sleeping in."

He riffled through a drawer in the dresser, grabbed a heather-gray T-shirt with the word ARMY written in bold letters across the front.

Kinsey smiled. "Thanks." And she disappeared into the bathroom, closing the door between them.

Sam paced the length of his room, imagining Kinsey stripping out of the dress and letting it fall to the floor around her ankles.

Heat washed through him.

Kinsey's mere presence would keep Sam tied in knots when he was supposed to be relaxing. He had to get rid of Kinsey. The sooner, the better. Otherwise, he'd be tempted to seduce her and spend the rest of the two weeks of enforced vacation in bed with the woman.

Assuming she was willing.

Oh, hell. What was he thinking? Kinsey had been through enough without having some horndog bastard taking advantage of her when she was at the lowest point in her life.

The shower went on in the other room, reminding Sam how Kinsey would be naked, standing beneath the spray, water running over her full breasts and down to the apex of her thighs.

Sam groaned and spun away from the door where he'd been standing, letting his mind run through every step the woman must be taking in the bathroom.

The walls of the room seemed to close in around Sam. He needed to get out in the open. Anytime he felt squeezed in, he only needed the liftoff of his helicopter to give his heart and mind the wings to escape the corner he'd been boxed into.

The shower shut off.

She'd be exiting the bathroom soon, wearing nothing but that damned Army T-shirt.

Sam was halfway to the door, determined to be out of the room when Kinsey emerged. He was reaching for the doorknob when the bathroom door opened.

"Sam?" her voice called out softly.

"Yeah." He turned, though he knew he shouldn't.

Kinsey stood framed in the bathroom door, wearing the T-shirt, her long, slim legs seeming to stretch all the way from her toes to her chin. She'd washed her hair and finger-combed it straight back from her forehead, making her appear even younger and more vulnerable. The style also exposed the long, regal line of her very kissable neck.

Sam ran his tongue across suddenly dry lips. "You can have the comforter from the bed," he said, his voice strained, his pulse slamming through his veins.

She frowned, her gaze darting to the door. "Are you going somewhere?"

The fear in Kinsey's voice gave Sam a jolt of guilt.

She'd been robbed, attacked and abandoned by her employers. With Sam walking out the door, she'd probably think he was abandoning her, as well.

"I'm going to the roof for a few minutes. The walls are closing in on me," he admitted. "I need air."

She nodded. "I know how you feel. I like to get outside when I'm stressed. Mind if I join you?"

Hell, she was the reason he needed to escape. Nonetheless, he heard the word, "Sure," come out of his mouth before he could think through his response. Once it was said, he was committed.

Damn.

She tugged at the hem of his T-shirt.

The garment covered her from her neck to halfway down her thighs, but it did nothing to quell the desire surging inside Sam.

If anything, that damned T-shirt looked sexy on Kinsey. Sexier than the cocktail dress. Perhaps because she couldn't be wearing anything beneath the shirt. She didn't have a spare pair of panties or a bra. Since she'd showered, she probably rinsed her underwear and hung them to dry for tomorrow.

Sam spun and jerked open the door, ready to run fast and far away from the woman standing behind him, practically naked. If he were a gentleman, he'd offer her a pair of his boxers. But his throat closed off, making it impossible for him to force air past his vocal cords.

He led the way to the patio and started to wave her up the ladder first. Thought better of the offer and climbed ahead of her. He wouldn't be able to concentrate on the rungs if he was behind her looking up, beneath the hem of the shirt.

God, he was lusting after a stranger and practically drooling over the potential sighting of a little naked ass. What did that make him? A pervert? Or a man who hadn't been laid in far too long?

His commander's words came back to him. Hadn't he told him to get laid?

On the way up the ladder, Sam paused to adjust himself in jeans that had become uncomfortably tight.

Kinsey would only be with him for the one night. She'd been through a lot, and she didn't need him coming on to her and making her feel threatened yet again.

Sam reached the rooftop, climbed out onto the surface and reached back to help Kinsey up the last few rungs.

She took his hand and let him guide her over the edge of the building and onto the roof, which had been converted into a patio, with decorative tile flooring. She teetered for a second, her foot catching on the last rung.

Still holding her hand, Sam jerked her into his arms and held her until she got her feet firmly planted.

"Sorry. I don't know why I'm so clumsy, lately." Kinsey's hands rested against his chest as she looked up into his eyes.

Starlight reflected off the light blue of her irises, making them shine.

Sam brushed a stray lock of blond hair off her forehead and tucked it behind her ear. "It's okay. You've had a rough day."

Kinsey stared up at him for a long moment, her gaze skimming over his face, pausing on his mouth. She drew in a deep breath, her breasts pressing into his chest. If he wasn't mistaken, the nipples had hardened and poked him gently.

Holy hell.

He let go of her suddenly and stepped away.

She swayed and would have fallen, but he reached out and steadied her, and then dropped his hand.

Turning away, he stared out over the view of Imerovigli, bathed in starlight, the whitewashed buildings glowing a soft blue. Lights from the many pools shone like turquoise gems terraced down the side of the hill.

"It's beautiful," Kinsey said, coming to stand beside him.

The clean scent of shampoo and soap drifted up from her wet head. A breeze stirred a few strands of hair that had already dried, lifting them up to flutter around her cheeks.

"Beautiful," Sam repeated, and then realized he wasn't looking at the cityscape, but at the woman standing at his side.

"I didn't have much of a view from my room. Not anything like this."

Sam chuckled. "I can barely see the courtyard from the bathroom in my room. I reserved this B&B because of this view. I didn't realize I'd have to scale a ladder to get to it."

"But the vistas from here are so worth it." She sighed. "I don't know how I'll manage to get myself out of the mess I'm in, but I can't regret coming to Santorini. If for nothing else, I'll always have this image in my memories."

Sam shook his head. "Are you always this upbeat about being robbed, attacked and abandoned?"

She looked up with a frown. "You saw me. I cried like a baby."

"But only for a minute. Then you were all happy again. I'd want to hit someone."

She faced the sea. "A person gains nothing by dwelling on the things they have no control over. I couldn't save my parents when they died in that car accident. But I know they wouldn't have wanted me to grieve away the rest of my life over their loss. They were firm believers in getting on with your life. Grieve, yes. Forever, no." She squared her shoulders and stared over the rooftops and the sea beyond. "I'll figure out a way to get back to the States. And, if not, I'll find work here in Greece."

"Without a passport and visa?"

She shrugged. "I'm nothing if not resilient."

For a few moments, he stood in silence. He liked that she didn't dwell on the negative and that she knew how to be lighthearted. He could use a dose of her optimism and calm in his life. His commander would like this woman. Hell, he was liking her far too much. "I'll buy your ticket back to the States," Sam said.

"What?" Kinsey dragged her gaze from the view and frowned up at him.

"You heard me right. I want to help."

Before he finished speaking, she was already shaking

her head. "No. I can't let you do that. I earn my way. I don't take charity."

"You can pay me back."

She frowned. "I might never see you again. How will I pay you back?"

"I'll leave you my address." Why was she being difficult? He was giving her a solution to her problem. One that would get her off the island and out of his life the soonest way possible. "You can send a check when you have the money, if it means that much to you to pay me back."

"No. I'll get a job and earn the money to buy my own ticket."

"Fine." The idea came to him in a flash. "I'll hire you."

Her frown deepened. "Hire me for what?" Then her eyes widened, and she backed away. "Look, I'm not that kind of woman. I don't trade sex for money."

Sam laughed out loud, and then clamped his hand over his mouth when he remembered they were probably above Mrs. D's bedroom. "Sweetheart, I don't need to pay women to have sex. They come willingly." He held up his hand to stop her next words. "I need a companion. Not one that sleeps in my bed, but one who will spend the days with me, go to dinner and maybe even be a dancing partner."

She stared at him in the starlight, her eyes wide, her brow wrinkled. "Why would you need to pay someone to do this? I'm sure you could find women who would line up to be with you."

"I don't want the hassle. All the work involved to get to know someone, or the trouble men have to go through to ask someone out. I have no intention of starting a relationship with a woman I will be leaving at the end of my stay. I just want to relax and take it easy while I'm here. No females stalking me. No commitment, just rest and relaxation. Having a woman with me will discourage those women standing in line for my company from coming on to me."

The frown remained etched on Kinsey's brow. "You want me to pretend to be your girl to keep other women at bay?"

"Yes. And I'll need pictures of us together to send to my commander."

"Whoa. Wait just a minute there." Shaking her head, she raised her hands. "I'm not into posing for porn."

"I'm not asking you to take nude pictures." Obviously, his jet lag impeded his ability to talk. He sighed. "My commander ordered me to rest and relax for two weeks, and he wants a daily report on how my kinks are unwinding. If I hire you to be my companion, you can help me prove to my commander I'm following his orders."

"Your commander can order you to have fun?" Kinsey's eyebrow rose. "They can do that?"

"He can. If I don't come back relaxed, he'll ground me from flying." The more the thought of the idea, the better he liked it. The only downside was he'd have to keep his hands off Kinsey. "So you see, you can help me out *and* earn your ticket back to the States in the process."

The frown descended again. "You're not pulling my leg, are you?"

Oh, he'd like to pull her very sexy leg and run his hands the length of both of them. "I'm not. This offer is legit. Do you accept?"

"And you don't want sex for the money you'll be paying me?"

"If I want sex, the activity has to be mutual with the party involved. No money will exchange hands."

"Good, because there will be no sex."

A stab of disappointment jabbed him in the groin. But he had to resist touching her or the arrangement would be the death of him. He held out his hand. "Deal?"

She hesitated a moment longer and then took his hand and shook it. "Deal."

"Good, tomorrow morning will be your first day on the job, and we're going shopping."

"Shopping?"

He grinned. "I can't have my girl running around in one of my T-shirts when we're supposed to be on vacation. And, as for that matter, we have to think about what to tell Mrs. D, the landlady."

She released his hand and rubbed hers on the T-shirt. "Will she have a problem with me staying in your room?"

"I'm almost positive she will, unless we go with what you told the hotel manager."

"I told him you were my fiancé just so he'd let you upstairs," she said.

"Then we'll tell Mrs. D the same. She shouldn't have a problem if she thinks we're engaged."

"Okay then," Kinsey smiled, her whole face shining in the starlight. "I have a job."

"And I have a decoy. These two weeks might not be as onerous as I originally thought." The solution was perfect. What could possibly go wrong?

Sam started down the ladder and realized to late that he should have let Kinsey go first. The entire way down, he fought to keep his gaze on the rungs, not on her perky bottom beneath the T-shirt.

Though she tugged at the hem with one hand to keep the fabric close around her, her efforts weren't enough.

Was he insane to think he could last two weeks without touching Kinsey? Oh, hell yeah.

5

Kinsey paced the floor of the little room she'd be sharing with Sam. She couldn't believe she had a solution to her problem. All she had to do was work for Sam for the next two weeks, and she'd earn the price of her flight back to the States.

Once there, she'd figure out how to start over with no money and no place to live. Maybe she could find a room in a homeless shelter until she landed a job and earned enough to put down deposits on an apartment.

But that would be when she arrived back in the States. For now, she had a job to do in Santorini, and she'd better do well to justify the pay. Plane tickets weren't cheap.

Working for Sam wouldn't be difficult if all she had to do was be a companion. She could make the reservations for their dinners and excursions, tidy his room and beat off all the women who would be vying for his attention. That shouldn't be too hard.

But, then again, he was a handsome man with all those muscles and a tight ass she was sure she could bounce a quarter off.

The trick would be to rein in her emotions and not let herself get attached. Two weeks was enough time to get to know someone and maybe even fall in love.

Not that she was ready to fall in love. Been there. Done that. Had the emotional baggage to prove it. She'd been in love with Travis Biggley back in Virginia. They dated for three years, long enough to know everything possible about each other.

At least, she thought so. What she didn't know was that he was seeing his secretary at the same time. When Kinsey pushed for the next step in their relationship, Travis said he needed time apart to think about what he wanted.

He took all of a day to ask his secretary to marry him. One day out of his relationship with Kinsey, and he was on his knee asking that little boyfriend-stealer to marry him.

That was when Kinsey pulled up all her stakes and moved to Greece. She'd put off living her life long enough for that man. She wasn't doing it any longer.

And she surely wasn't falling in love with a guy who'd just told her he wasn't interested in commitment. That's why he'd hired her. To keep women off his scent. All women—including her.

Having sworn off men for the near future, she shouldn't have a problem keeping her hands off the sexy helicopter pilot.

They tiptoed back through the hallway and into Sam's room.

"I'm getting a shower. Help yourself to the blanket on the bed." And Sam entered the bathroom, closing the door between them.

Once he was out of sight, she could finally take a deep breath.

Sam Magnus was a man's man and hard to miss or ignore. His dark hair and blue eyes made him even more mysterious and attractive.

Kinsey would have her hands full beating back the women. She curled her fingers into her palms, making tight fists. Those women wouldn't get within two feet of her man. Her man. Ha! So, he wasn't *her* man. But she'd play her part to the T and make the ladies believe she was the fiancée of the handsome American soldier.

The scent of food made Kinsey pause at the little table and lift a dishtowel to discover a plate of food.

Her stomach rumbled. She'd spent the day snorkeling, had been kidnapped and never had supper.

She glanced toward the bathroom door. Would Sam mind if she had just a little bit of his dinner?

Kinsey inhaled the rich aroma of a traditional Greek meal, fighting the urge to sneak a bite. She'd only have a little. Enough to take the edge off her hunger.

She sat at the table and ate half of the casserole-like dish on the plate before she could stop.

Sam stuck his head through the door. "Mrs. D left a plate of moussaka on the table. I've already eaten. Help yourself."

Kinsey swallowed the bite she'd been chewing, heat rising into her cheeks. "Thanks."

The door closed again and Kinsey finished off the food on the plate. She sat back in her chair, full of great food and feeling a little better about her situation.

The sound of water spraying in the bathtub drew her attention to the bathroom door. Not that she could see through the wood paneling, but she had an imagination and it was running wild with images of Sam standing naked beneath the water.

Crap! What was she thinking? The man was her employer, not her lover or her fiancé. She'd better keep that in mind at all times, or her naughty thoughts would land her in hotter water than she'd already been scalded by.

Rather than take the comforter from the bed, Kinsey checked in the closet and found a spare blanket. She sat in the overstuffed chair, plumped the down pillow and pulled the blanket up around her. The air in the room was really too warm for a covering of any kind, so she dropped it to her waist and curled her feet under her.

The chair didn't have enough room for her to stretch out, but it would have to do. She was lucky to have a roof over her head and a safe haven from kidnappers. She wouldn't complain.

The sound of the shower shutting off in the other room made Kinsey's heart skip several beats. Would Sam come out of the bathroom fully clothed, or would he just wrap a towel around his narrow hips and walk his sexy body out into the bedroom? Which begged the next question...did he sleep nude?

Kinsey's cheeks burned at the thought. She'd known the guy less than a couple hours, but she was already drooling over his body and dreaming about him strutting his stuff in the buff.

The bathroom door opened, and Sam emerged wearing a pair of gym shorts and an old T-shirt. "For the record, I sleep in the nude."

Kinsey gasped, her cheeks scorching. "I didn't ask."

"I'm just telling you because I'm making an exception and wearing shorts to bed, to spare you any embarrassment."

"You won't embarrass me. You don't have anything I haven't seen." She tried for nonchalance, when in fact, she had trouble breathing at the thought of Sam naked.

"Still, as your boss, I don't want to make you uncomfortable."

"This is your room. I'm only here, because I have nowhere else to go. You can do whatever you want. Please yourself. I'm not paying the bill." She lay back and closed her eyes, feigning sleep. "Good night, Mr. Magnus."

"Sam," he corrected. "We're supposed to be engaged."

She nodded. "Yes, sir." She popped a salute and smiled. "Goodnight, Mr....Sam."

He frowned. "Will you be all right in that chair?"

"Don't worry about me. I'll be fine. It's better than sleeping on a sandy beach or in an alley on stone steps."

"Yeah, but you're knotted up like a pretzel."

"I'm very flexible." Again, she closed her eyes. "Goodnight, Sam."

"Goodnight, Kinsey."

"Thank you for saving my life," she added softly.

"You're welcome." He turned off the light on his nightstand and the bedsprings creaked as he settled on the mattress.

A few minutes passed before Kinsey's eyes adjusted to the limited starlight creeping through the one window in the room.

Sam pulled his T-shirt over his head and draped it across the white iron headboard.

The starlight that managed to find its way into the room bathed his shoulders and chest in a dark, blue-gray hue.

Kinsey couldn't stop staring from beneath her lashes. Yes, keeping from falling for such a man would be difficult for most women. But she had the track record of falling in love with the wrong man. She wouldn't be so gullible next time. No. There wouldn't be a next time.

She adjusted her limbs, searching for a comfortable position, and resigned herself to a restless night's sleep. Tomorrow had to be a better day than the one she'd barely survived.

SAM LAY back on the mattress and stared up at the ceiling, hyper-aware of the woman wearing his T-shirt in the chair not six feet away.

Like he'd guessed, she'd rinsed her undergarments and hung them to dry in the bathroom.

That meant she was naked beneath the T-shirt. Her

bare breasts and lady parts were touching the soft jersey fabric.

An ache built at Sam's core. He'd gone far too long without a woman. But now was not the time to get involved. Especially with Kinsey. She was heading back to the States to start her life over. He was scheduled to return to Afghanistan for the next three months.

Maybe he shouldn't have hired her to fend off the ladies on the island. He might have set himself up for a lot more frustration than he planned for. Then again, he would satisfy his commander's demand to chill out. What better way to prove to the boss that he was enjoying his vacation than by sending the man pictures of him snorkeling, swimming and dancing with a beautiful woman?

Sam lay for a while longer, analyzing the events of the evening. Who were the men who'd attempted to kidnap Kinsey, and where had they been taking her? If Kinsey had been telling the truth about working as an au pair for the Martins, why had the couple ditched her and left three weeks early? And why would the hotel deny all knowledge that she'd been a guest there?

None of these incidents were making sense. Either the staff at the hotel were in on some massive lie, or Kinsey had been given a lot more of the knock-out drug than Sam first assumed.

The hours ticked by, and Sam remained awake, his mind going over and over the fight and the hotel staff's reaction to Kinsey's claims she'd been registered there.

The woman in question moaned softly and squirmed in the tight confines of the armchair.

Sam pushed up on his elbows and studied her from across the room.

She was asleep, but apparently having a nightmare, which was to be expected. The woman had been attacked and overpowered by two men. More than likely, she'd have nightmares for the rest of her life. His heart squeezed inside his chest. No woman should be treated the way those men had handled her.

Kinsey moaned again and kicked out. The movement sent her flying out of the chair to land hard on the floor. She woke with a start, her eyelids fluttering. "Oh!"

Sam flew out of the bed and dropped to his knees beside her. "Are you okay?" He slipped an arm around her back and one beneath her legs.

"What?" She blinked again and shoved at Sam, her eyes wide, her body tense. "Where am I? What's happening?"

"You're okay." He lifted her up against him and stood. "You're in my room. You must have had a bad dream."

She stared into his eyes for a long moment, and then her body relaxed. "Oh, it's you, Sam." She wrapped one arm around his neck and leaned her face into his shoulder, her eyes closing. Her other hand rested on his chest, her fingers digging into his flesh. "Those men came back for me."

"Only in your nightmare. I won't let them get to you," he reassured her. "You're safe with me."

She sighed. "Thank you." And she was asleep again.

Sam remained standing with her in his arms, liking the way she felt so warm and soft against his body. But he couldn't hold her all night. He glanced at the chair. How would he fit her back in that small space? She'd already fallen out once. If he laid her there, she'd just roll out again.

His gaze moved to the bed. What the hell? She could sleep on the bed with him. He'd keep his hands to himself and get up before she did so that she didn't think he was coming on to her.

Then again, he could sleep in the chair…

Nope. He was a big guy. He was supposed to be in Greece to relax. Sleeping in a chair would not accomplish that goal.

Too tired to analyze his motives, he carried Kinsey to the bed, laid her down on the mattress and pulled up the blanket over her bare legs.

The shirt had hiked up to her hip in the process. The skin was milky white above her bikini line.

The sudden urge to kiss her there nearly overwhelmed him. Sam moaned softly, careful not to wake Kinsey. He piled pillows in a line down the middle of the bed and rounded the corner of the mattress to lie on the other side.

He could do this and not succumb to his baser needs. Kinsey needed sleep. She'd been through a lot and still had more to deal with the following day.

Sam needed sleep, too. He shot a look at his watch on the nightstand. Well into the wee hours of the morning, he wouldn't get many hours of shut-eye before he had to rise ahead of Kinsey.

Closing his eyes, he tried to think of anything other than the beautiful woman lying in the bed next to him.

Well, almost next to him. If he didn't count the pillows.

For a long time, he lay awake, fighting his rising desire and losing horribly. If his lust for her wasn't bad enough, he worried someone would come back for her while he slept. Sam reached beneath the pillows and found Kinsey's hand. He tucked it into his and held on. If one of those men traced her to this room and broke in while he slept, they wouldn't get her away.

When Sam thought he'd never drift off into much-needed sleep, he finally did. And with sleep came his own nightmares of men stealing Kinsey and carrying her off to an unknown dark and terrible place.

SUN SHINING into the little window over the bed brought Sam back to reality the next morning. He looked at his watch and realized he'd slept well past the usual hour he rose.

Something warm and soft pressed against his side. He glanced down to see Kinsey's arm draped across his middle and her head resting against his chest. The wall of pillows between them had migrated to the bottom of the bed.

How the hell could he extricate himself without waking the woman? She'd think he'd taken advantage of her. And in his mind, he had, though he'd never acted on his lusty thoughts.

He lay for a long moment, inhaling the scent of the shampoo in her hair and the sweet smell of her skin. Sam ached to hold her, to run his hand over her soft skin and to kiss her lips. All things he couldn't do. The woman was asleep, for heaven's sake.

Kinsey stirred, her hand curling against his skin.

His groin tightened. If he didn't want to suffer the wrath of an angry woman, he had to move before she woke. Careful not to disturb her, he gently slid her arm off his chest, lifted her head and scooted his shoulder from beneath it, replacing it with a pillow. Then he rolled out of the bed and stood.

Kinsey's eyes remained closed, her breathing deep and steady.

Sam let go of the breath he'd held, grabbed clothes from the dresser and retreated to the bathroom where he brushed his teeth, washed his face and combed his hair. Long strands of blond hair hung in his comb, but he didn't mind.

When he was fully clothed, he opened the door to find Kinsey attempting to zip the back of her dress.

"Why are you wearing that?" he asked, remembering the fact her bra and panties were still hanging in the bathroom. Which meant she was naked beneath the dress. He swallowed a groan.

Kinsey dropped the hand she had behind her back and sighed. "It's the only thing I have."

"You could wear one of my shirts and a pair of my shorts. They'll be big, but I'm sure we can secure them to keep them from falling off."

She smiled. "If it's all the same to you, I prefer my own clothes. And I have every intention of recovering my belongings."

He shrugged. "Have it your way, but I'm buying you a pair of shoes before we go too far today."

Kinsey grimaced. "I keep saying this, but it's true... I'll pay you back."

"I'm not as worried about your paying me back as I am about you tearing up your feet because you're too proud to admit you need help."

"Trust me, I'll swallow my pride for a pair of sandals."

He nodded, glad she wasn't fighting him on this one item. "Hurry in the bathroom, I'm sure Mrs. D doesn't like to be kept waiting to serve her guests breakfast."

Kinsey entered the bathroom, closed the door and was back out, combed, face shiny and smooth and frowning. "How will you explain me to your landlady?"

"I'm telling her you arrived late at night, that your plane was delayed and you caught a ride with a fishing boat from the mainland."

"And my lack of shoes and luggage?"

"Your luggage will be delivered when the plane catches up, and you lost your shoes on board the fishing vessel. Do I have to think of everything?" He winked.

"Just making sure our stories match." She tipped her head toward the bathroom. "I hope you don't mind that I used your comb and some of your toothpaste."

He shrugged. "As long as you didn't use my toothbrush, we're all good." He didn't like that she thought of herself as a burden. "We can get you some toiletries when we shop for your shoes."

"At least a toothbrush," Kinsey agreed. "I can't finger brush my teeth for long before they start falling out."

"Shall we?" He held open the door and waited for her to pass through. Then he stepped in front of her and led the way to the dining room where Mrs. Demopolis had small bistro tables decorated with colorfully patterned tablecloths. Fresh bread rested in baskets on each, along with glasses of orange juice.

The landlady backed through a swinging door carrying a teapot. "Oh, very good. You are here. Sit anywhere. I will serve your tea."

"Thank you, Mrs. D. But I'd prefer coffee. However, my fiancée might prefer tea." He stepped to the side, allowing the older woman a chance to see he was not alone.

Kinsey gave the woman a wan smile and wiggled her fingers in a little wave. "Hello. I'm Kinsey, Sam's... fiancée."

Mrs. D's eyes widened. and her gaze shifted from Kinsey to Sam and back to Kinsey. "What is this? You didn't say in your reservation two would be in the room."

Kinsey chuckled. "I surprised him. When I learned he would be in Santorini, I couldn't pass up the opportunity to see him. I've been working in Athens for the past month and haven't seen Sam that whole time."

"So," Sam picked up the story, "Kinsey jumped on a plane and flew out to see me."

"Only my plane didn't make it off the ground. It was delayed, so I took the train to the coast and hired a boat to ferry me out to the island." She smiled. "I hope you don't mind. I promise not to be messy or loud."

"Oh, there is no problem. I will add extra towels and

pillows to the room." Mrs. D glanced from Sam to Kinsey. "I did not know Mr. Magnus was engaged to be married." She grinned at Sam, set the teapot on a table and grabbed his hands. "I am happy for you both." Her gaze took in both Sam and Kinsey. "She is very beautiful. You two will make pretty babies."

Sam's cheeks heated. The thought of making babies with Kinsey brought up very lustful images in his head. "Thank you, Mrs. D."

"Now, sit. Sit." She waved her arms expansively. "You must be hungry after spending the night in the arms of your lover."

Kinsey's cheeks brightened with color. "Oh. Yes. Of course."

"Will you have tea or coffee?" their hostess asked.

"Tea for me," Kinsey replied. "I can serve myself." She lifted the teapot, poured hot water into a cup and placed a teabag in the steaming liquid.

Mrs. D hurried back to the kitchen, muttering about making up an additional plate of food.

Sam breathed a sigh, glad his hostess had been so welcoming to Kinsey. He held out a chair. "Please, have a seat."

Kinsey carried her teacup to the table and sat, allowing Sam to scoot her chair beneath her.

When he'd settled, she leaned across the table. "Think she bought it?" she whispered.

"Hook, line and sinker," Sam said with a grin.

"I hope she doesn't ask a lot of questions. I'm not very good at lying," Kinsey said.

"Don't worry. I'm sure she has many more things to

do than to question ladies about their reasons for showing up in the middle of the night."

"She's the owner of a B&B, I'm sure she'll be curious." Kinsey tucked her bare feet beneath her chair and dipped a teabag into her cup.

The door to the kitchen swung open again, and Mrs. D entered the dining room carrying a large tray loaded with food. "I will make more eggs and toast, if this is not enough."

Kinsey looked at the spread of meat, cheeses, tomatoes, scrambled eggs and beans. "This is way more than enough. Will others be joining us?"

The older woman shook her head. "The others have all eaten and checked out. You two are the last to come to breakfast."

"We'll be on time tomorrow," Sam assured her. That there would be a tomorrow with Kinsey, struck Sam as strange. Now that she was working for him, he had her exclusively until his two weeks were up, and he could return to his unit.

Kinsey dug into the food, loading her plate with eggs, toast, bacon and bread rolls.

"I'm glad to see you're not one of those women who only nibble."

Kinsey gave him a twisted smile. "I don't normally pick at my food, but I *am* hungry."

Sam chuckled. "The moussaka last night wasn't enough?"

"Oh, it was wonderful, but that was last night."

"I would think after what happened, you'd be too nervous to eat."

She snorted. "When I'm nervous, I eat." As if to prove her words, she ate until she cleaned her plate and laughed. "With my luck, I never know when I'll get another meal."

"Stick with me. I don't miss chow." Sam pushed back from the table. "Did you get enough?"

"More than enough."

"Then let's go find you some shoes and clothes."

"And my suitcase," Kinsey added.

"And your suitcase." Sam held out his hand. "Come on, fiancée, we have a lot to accomplish before I check in with my commander. I can't have him thinking you only have one dress in your wardrobe. He might get suspicious. And we have to plan some activities to look like I'm having fun and relaxing."

"I can take pictures if you have a camera and schedule excursions like snorkeling, scuba and sailing."

"You're on. As soon as we get you outfitted." Sam grinned, gripped her elbow and led her toward the exit. "Hell, I'd stand on my head and do back handsprings if it means keeping my flight status. We need to get moving."

The sooner they started sending the *proof* of his relaxing vacation to Colonel Cooley, the better off he'd be. With a plan in place to keep his commander placated, he really could relax and enjoy the rest of his mandated time on the island. Then he could get back to the real work of flying helicopters into the war zones of Afghanistan, Iraq or wherever the hell they were sending the Spec Ops guys.

6

THEY HIKED HALFWAY through the village before they found any shops selling shoes and clothing.

Kinsey was ready for a pair of shoes to save her feet from the small stones she inevitably found when she was least expecting them. Her heels bruised and cut, she gladly sat in a chair. Thankfully, the shop keeper gave her a cloth to wipe her dirty feet before she tried on shoes. Eventually, she found a pair of sandals that would protect the soles of her feet and still go with most anything she might wear from casual to dressy.

Once they had her shoes, she stepped out of the store and glanced up to where the Porto Takisi stood. "Now we can go retrieve my suitcase."

"Not yet." Sam hooked her elbow and guided her into a store selling classy shorts, skirts and blouses.

Kinsey took one look at the price tags, bit back a gasp, and crossed her arms over her chest. "No. I can't afford these clothes."

"I can, and I need you to look like you're on vacation."

"I can find a thrift store and accomplish the same goals at a tenth of the cost," she insisted.

"On Santorini?" Sam shook his head. "Humor me. I really need my commander to believe I have a girlfriend and not a homeless person."

"Don't knock the homeless," she grumbled. "We don't all get in these situations because we want be homeless," she said softly.

He captured her hands in his. "I know. And I'm not making fun of you. I want you to appear as happy and carefree as I do. And you can't do that in a torn cocktail dress." He selected several blouses, shorts and skirts, piled them in her arms and sent her toward the changing rooms. "I want to see what they look like on you."

"Seriously? Are you getting a little too personal with your new assistant?" she said, half-joking. Travis had never asked her to model clothes for him. A trickle of excitement ran through her.

"I'm the boss, which means I'm calling the shots. If you can't stand the heat, maybe this deal isn't for you." He crossed his arms over his chest. "What's it to be? Clothes, or back out on the street? I need an assistant and companion. If you won't do it, I'll find someone who will."

"Fine. I'll do it." She shuffled off to the changing room. As she entered, she glanced over her shoulder to where Sam was taking a seat in front of the three-way mirror.

She shook her head and hurried inside. If he wanted a fashion show, she'd give it to him. He was paying for her ticket back to the States, so why was she arguing with the man?

One by one, she tried on the outfits. When she stepped out, Sam gave her a thumbs-up or a thumbs-down gesture. They settled on four blouses, two pairs of shorts, a bikini that made Kinsey blush when she stepped out of the dressing room, and a long skirt she could wear out to dinner. They went next door to complete her wardrobe with underwear, a new bra and accessories. On their way back to the Porto Takisi, they found a store selling toiletries where Sam bought her a toothbrush, hairbrush and makeup.

"Not that you need it," Sam assured her.

When she asked for the receipts, she practically had her hand slapped by her boss.

"Consider the clothes and supplies as part of your pay."

"If you spend all your money on this stuff, you won't have enough left to purchase my airline ticket back to the States."

"I have enough," Sam announced. "In the past eight years, I've been on active duty, I never use all of my leave, and I'm never home long enough to spend the money I earn."

Kinsey wished she could claim she was as financially secure. She had used most of her savings to pay for her flight to Greece. What little she'd had left was gone with her backpack. She admired a man who managed his money.

Travis had been a big spender, running up credit card debt with no thought as to how he'd pay it off.

At least Kinsey didn't have any debt. Except what she now owed Sam. She sighed. She'd pay him back if she had to sell her organs to do it.

Less than an hour later, she walked out of the shopping center with several large bags of clothing and wearing a casual, sky-blue sundress and the new sandals. "When we get my suitcase, we can return some of these items."

"You will not."

Kinsey frowned. "But I won't have room in my case for the new clothes."

"Then we'll get you an additional suitcase."

"I can't afford to pay you back of all of these items."

"I told you, I'm including them as part of your pay. Consider it a bonus."

"But I haven't done anything to earn it yet," she argued.

"After we hit the Porto Takisi, I want you to organize a snorkeling excursion, and we'll need an underwater camera."

"I can set up that activity." They passed a shop with dive and snorkeling equipment. Kinsey ducked in, selected a disposable underwater camera and a couple of large beach towels.

Sam paid for the items and carried the bag out of the shop. "Now, you're getting the hang of spending my money. Like a proper fiancée."

Kinsey felt bad about being so easy with his credit

cards. "If you think anything is too much, just tell me. I don't want the bank to block your account."

"I was just kidding." Sam took one of the bags from her, lightening her load. "Let's run these back to our room before we hit the Takisi."

Kinsey agreed, wanting to have her hands free for when she confronted the staff at Porto Takisi about her belongings.

After they dropped off her new clothes and the beach towels and made their way to the hotel, the time was getting close to noon. The act was almost surreal stepping into the lobby of the place where she'd spent the past week with a family that hadn't had the decency to pay her before they skipped town.

"I hope we have better luck with the day staff than we did with the night shift." Kinsey squared her shoulders and marched past the empty concierge desk to registration. Kinsey didn't recognize the woman behind the counter, but that fact didn't slow her down. "I'd like to speak with the manager."

"Is there something I can help you with?" the clerk asked.

"Nope," Kinsey said. "I need the manager."

"I'm sorry, miss. But the manager is not available," the clerk said.

"Then get me the president or the CEO or someone in charge." Kinsey congratulated herself on how calm she was at delivering her demand.

"Miss, those people are not available at this time. They had a big meeting on the mainland, and the management team left this morning to attend."

"Seriously?" Kinsey gritted her teeth to keep from screaming. "What time do you expect them to return?"

"Late this evening, miss." The clerk glanced over her shoulder. "If that's all you want, could you step aside so I might assist another customer?"

"Maybe you can help me, after all," Kinsey said. "Will you check and see if I have a reservation for a room here?"

"Name, please?"

"Kinsey Phillips." Kinsey waited while the clerk ran her fingers over the keyboard.

Moments later, the woman shook her head. "I'm sorry, miss, but no one is registered under that name."

Anger roiled in Kinsey's belly. "Did I ever have a reservation here?" she asked. "Check for yesterday, and the entire week before."

The woman clicked the keys and finally shook her head. "I show no record of you having stayed at this hotel last week." She glanced up. "Is there a problem?"

"If I had a problem, would you be able to fix it?" Kinsey drew in a deep breath and let it out. "Never mind." Spinning on the smooth tile floor, she headed back toward the exit, stopping when she came to the concierge's desk.

Sam kept pace with her, standing beside her as she addressed the man with his back to her.

"Excuse me," Kinsey said.

Giorgio had been the concierge for the past week, there early in the morning, and staying until late at night. He'd been cordial, friendly and the one person Kinsey felt comfortable talking with other than the Martins. The man at the desk wasn't Giorgio.

"Miss, can I help you?"

"Yes, you can." Kinsey fought feelings of hopelessness and disappointment. Self-pity would accomplish nothing. "You can tell me where I can find Giorgio."

He blinked and tipped his head to one side. "Excuse me?"

"Giorgio, the concierge. Will he be in to work today?"

"I am the concierge," the man said, pressing a hand to his chest. "How might I help you?"

"You can help by telling me where to find Giorgio."

The concierge frowned. "Pardon me, miss. No one by the name of Giorgio works at this hotel."

"Was he fired?" Kinsey asked.

The concierge shook his head. "No, miss. I have been the concierge for the past seven years."

Kinsey glared at the man. He was lying. He had to be. She searched his face, looking for some indication he wasn't telling the truth, but he appeared sincere. "Then where were you last week when Giorgio was working this desk?"

"I'm sorry, miss, but you must be mistaken. Perhaps hotel security can help you." He waved to a man dressed in a gray suit across the room.

"Time to go." Sam hooked her elbow and steered her toward the exit. "You heard the manager last night. He said he'd have us arrested for trespassing if we showed up today."

Her thoughts swirling, Kinsey dug in her heels,

refusing to go another step. "But I don't have my things."

"I don't think you'll win this argument, and I won't have an easy time of it explaining to my commander why I'm sitting in a jail cell because I was trespassing."

She didn't want to put Sam in a bind, or she would have stood up for herself and demanded to know where they'd placed her clothes, toiletries and photos. She wasn't asking for anything else, only the things that belonged to her.

With a security guy closing in on them, she couldn't take that risk when her actions could impact Sam. Kinsey marched out the door and into the street. "What else can I do, other than search the entire hotel to find my things?"

"We can come back later when the management team returns from their big meeting," Sam suggested.

Kinsey's eyes narrowed. "I don't know why they're lying or going to such great lengths to hide the fact I was here and staying in that suite. Yeah, we'll be back later. I want to speak with the manager, the manager's manager, and anyone else who might have the balls to tell me the truth." That suitcase contained her last connection to her parents. She had to find it.

Sam drew her hand through the crook of his elbow. "But for now, let's go to the beach."

Kinsey clamped her mouth shut to keep from screaming. How could she go to the beach and act like nothing was wrong, when all of Santorini seemed to be plotting against her?

She had to remember Sam was her ticket home. All

she had to do was be his companion for the next two weeks, and he'd buy her that plane ticket to a new life.

Ha! That had been her original plan coming to Greece. A new life. An escape from the dead-end relationship she'd wasted three of the best years of her life on.

The promise of a job had fallen through, then the Martins had skipped out without paying her. Her track record of judging peoples' characters wasn't all that good. She stopped before she'd gone more than three yards with Sam. "You're not ducking out on me at the last minute, are you?"

He stared at her, a frown denting his forehead. "What do you mean?"

"I mean, I spent an entire week looking after the Martin's kids and they left without paying me what I was owed."

"I told you, I'll buy your ticket today. But you wanted to earn it. If it makes you feel better, I'll purchase the ticket, hand it over to you, and let you decide if you're staying for the two weeks or going back to the States." He patted her hand. "How's that?"

Some of the tension drained, and she started walking again. "I guess that would be okay. I'm sorry. You've been amazing, and I'm being ungrateful."

"Don't knock yourself. I'd be skeptical, too, if I was in your predicament. Let's go back to the room, change into beach clothes and I'll make that reservation. And, hopefully, Mrs. D will have a printer we can use to print out a copy."

"Thank you." Kinsey squeezed his arm. "And we'll be

sure to take some awesome pictures for your commander."

"I'm counting on it. The sooner I convince him that I'm taking it easy, the more likely he'll get off my back."

They'd gone around a corner, out of sight of the hotel when a dark-haired young woman stepped out of the shadows, carrying a suitcase.

Kinsey recognized her as Leora, the maid who'd taken care of the Martins' and her room for the past week. The case in her hand had a bright red, polka-dot ribbon tied to the handle.

Joy filled Kinsey's heart. "That's my suitcase!"

Leora didn't put up a fight when Kinsey grabbed the case and clutched it to her chest. "Where did you get this?"

The young woman's gaze darted left and right. She ducked back into a shadowy gap between buildings and motioned for Kinsey and Sam to join her. When they did, she whispered. "You must leave, now."

"So, they are lying." Kinsey's hands balled into fists. "Why?"

Leora twisted her fingers together. "They will be unhappy if they know I gave you this suitcase. Please, you must leave Santorini now."

"But why would they tell me I wasn't a guest there?"

"Not all is as it appears," Leora said. "Stay away from Porto Takisi." Then she was gone, slipping through the shadows and disappearing around a corner.

"What the hell just happened?" Kinsey said, her gaze following Leora. "Why would the hotel staff lie to my face and tell me I'd never been to that hotel?"

"I don't know, but we should take the woman's advice and get as far away from the place as we can." He took the suitcase from her, hooked her arm and led her away, glancing over his shoulder several times as they worked their way back to his B&B.

Kinsey noted the direction they were headed was a little more convoluted than the route they'd taken the night before. "Why are we going a different way?"

"If anyone is following you, you don't want to establish a routine. Doing so makes it too easy for them to lay in wait and nab you when you least expect it. When you vary your route, you keep your pursuers guessing."

At his serious tone, Kinsey shivered. "You think someone might follow me?" She couldn't imagine why anyone would think she was that important. "Why? I'm not from a rich family. I'd make a terrible hostage. My parents are dead and didn't leave me any money."

"You're blond and female," Sam said, his tone flat. "You're worth a lot on the sex market."

Kinsey gasped and ground to a halt. "You think those two guys who tried to kidnap me were taking me to some sex market?"

Jaw clenched, Sam nodded. "Most likely."

"That's insane."

"It's big business and happens all too often to lone females. Not only in foreign countries, but in the U.S. The military requires every soldier to attend briefings on human trafficking to be aware and observant, as well as to report any possible human trafficking rings."

Kinsey pressed a hand to her chest. "I guess I've known about the horrible practice, but I never thought it could happen to me." She glanced around. Suddenly, the bright, cheerful white walls of the city seemed to be riddled with shadows. Shadows that could be harboring dark-hearted men waiting to snatch unsuspecting women to sell to disgusting human brokers.

She leaned into Sam, glad for his protection and the solidity of his muscles. He could fight off any attacker. Her training in self-defense seemed almost laughable. The two men, with minimal effort, had overcome her pitiful attempts to fight back. Having Sam at her side gave her a great sense of security she wouldn't have had otherwise.

She'd sure as hell stick to him for the duration of her stay on Santorini. She did not want to end up on some auctioneer's dais, stripped, drugged and sold for sex.

7

SAM KEPT Kinsey close as he zigzagged through the alleyways, choosing an alternate route back to his B&B.

He suspected staff members at the Porto Takisi had been involved in the attempted abduction of the pretty blonde. The Martins sounded as if they might have been in on the plot, as well. Why else would they leave when they did, with no message or reason left behind to explain their sudden need to exit the island?

The whole elaborate plan made Sam uneasy. If they went to that much effort and staged the plot over a week just to snatch Kinsey, wouldn't they try again?

When he reached the B&B, Sam insisted on entering the room first. He took a moment to search the closet, bathroom and beneath the bed.

"What are you looking for?" Kinsey asked, stepping into the room behind him.

"Intruders." He rose to his feet after looking beneath the bed.

Kinsey's pretty pink lips quirked. "Did you find any in this tiny room?"

"Don't laugh." He rubbed the side of his head where she'd hit him with the bar of soap. "You got the better of me in the bathroom just last night."

She cringed. "I did, didn't I? Sorry. I thought you were one of the men who'd knocked me out."

"I get that. No harm, no foul. But I'm not too happy about what happened at the hotel, either." He set the suitcase on the bed. Then he dug his laptop out of the top drawer of the dresser and laid it on the small table. "I'm making that reservation for you now. That way you know I'm legit about this deal."

"I'm sorry I doubted you."

"Don't be." He sat and punched the start key. "Where do you want to land in the States?"

"Norfolk, Virginia. It's the only home I've ever known. Not that I have a place to go back to. But it'll be a start."

"No house or apartment?" Even he had an apartment in the States, though he was rarely there. If he had someone like Kinsey waiting for him, he'd be more inclined to go home.

She shook her head. "I sold everything. I intended to work in Greece for the next year and save money to move on to another country after that."

"Can't you still follow that plan?"

Her lips twisted. "Getting laid off before I started my job and then mugged in Athens, and having all my money and identification stolen, kind of took the joy out of that plan."

His chest tight, Sam connected to the internet and found the best deal on a ticket back to Virginia. "Do you have friends you can stay with when you get back?"

Kinsey pulled up a chair beside hm. "My ex-boyfriend pretty much cut me off from what few friends I had."

Sam's fists tightened. Her ex must have been real a jerk. "What about your old job? Can you go back to that?"

She shook her head. "No. I worked as a bookkeeper for a man who retired the day I left." She laughed. "He didn't want to have to train another bookkeeper. He's living in Cabo San Lucas now. But don't worry. I know my way around Norfolk. I'll be okay. And I really appreciate your doing this for me."

Sam didn't like that she had nowhere to go, and no one to stay with. But she had her plan and he'd promised her a ticket back.

With Kinsey looking over his shoulder, Sam spent the next few minutes finding a flight departing the same day he was scheduled on the same plane from Santorini. At least he'd see her to the Athens airport before they split up to go their separate ways.

Once he had the flight reserved, he called Mrs. D on the house phone, asked for the password and connected to her printer in the common area. "We can pick up your ticket information when we pass through."

Kinsey smiled. "Thank you. It's nice to have one hurdle cleared on the road to my recovery. And I can't tell you how happy I am that I got back my suitcase."

She crossed to the bed, unzipped the case and opened it. Then she riffled through the contents.

The items appeared to have been thrown in, with no care taken to fold the clothing or organize the content. Kinsey didn't seem to notice. She shoved her way through, tossing loose items to the side until she reached something at the bottom. When she brought it out, Sam could see that she held a picture frame. "Is that your family?" Sam asked.

Kinsey glanced down at the image of a man with a woman who had blond hair and blue eyes just like Kinsey's.

Sam almost mistook her for Kinsey, except the girl standing in front of the couple had Kinsey's eyes and her open smile. A younger version of the woman beside him in the B&B.

"We were at the beach when this picture was taken. My father liked taking us to the ocean for our holidays. We lived in Virginia. Driving to Virginia Beach or further south to Myrtle Beach in South Carolina wasn't too hard." She stared down at the smiling family. "Sometimes, I feel like this photo is my last tangible connection to them."

"Your parents will always be alive in your memories. The good ones never go away," Sam said. And the bad ones. But he didn't say that.

"I know that. And I have some digital photos stored online, but this physical photograph reminds me so much of how hopeful and in love they were. I always wanted what they had."

The longing in her voice tugged at Sam's heart. His

parents had been like that. He'd thought he would be, too. He'd gone so far as to fall in love with a woman early in his Army career. They got engaged, and then he'd watched as cancer sucked the life out of her. "Sometimes things don't turn out the way we think they should. Some events make you stronger."

"Or make you run away from everything you knew," she whispered. "To get away from the disappointment life has left you with."

Sam nodded, staring down at the picture in Kinsey's hand but seeing an image of Leigha as she lay in her hospital bed, her body wasted away, her glorious hair gone, and eyes sunken. She'd clung to life until no more life existed to cling to. Then she'd said goodbye and slipped away.

That's when he'd run away. Away from the dream of having someone in his life and of establishing a home filled with kids.

The last mission he'd flown had been on the second anniversary of Leigha's death. He should have known better than to fly that night. His heart had been heavy with resurfacing grief. He'd run...or flown into enemy territory, chased by the demons of his past. He couldn't fly fast enough to escape the truth. She wasn't coming back, and if they did it all again, he couldn't have changed anything to save her.

"Hey."

A hand touched his arm, bringing him back to the present.

Kinsey stared up at him. "Are you okay?"

He shook himself out of his morose memories. "Yeah. Why do you ask?"

"You looked like you'd just lost your best friend."

"I did." He turned away and grabbed a pair of swim trunks from the dresser with the intention of changing in the bathroom.

Kinsey stood between him and his destination. "Do you want to talk about it?" She gave him a gentle smile. "After all, I'm your companion. I'm here for you."

Heart aching, he shook his head. "Nothing to talk about."

Kinsey stared into his eyes. "I think there is, but if you're not ready, I won't push." She grinned up at him. "I'm here all week. We'll have time."

He stepped around her, a spark of anger surging through him. What business did this stranger have digging into his past? Leigha was none of Kinsey's business, and he had no intention of discussing his fiancée's death with the woman. As he walked into the bathroom, he heard her voice behind him.

"We both seem to have memories we are running from. I just think it might help to share. You know, get our troubles off our chests. Those things we bury deep inside tend to fester and eventually bubble to the surface in the most regrettable ways."

Sam spun to face Kinsey. "Some things are private. You're not a shrink, I'm not your pet project. You're a paid companion, not a friend or even a real fiancée. I had one once, and she was perfect." He turned away, determined to get to the bathroom before he said anything more. He was already regretting telling her anything about his Leigha.

"If she was so perfect, where is she now?" Kinsey asked, her tone soft, her voice carrying because of the content, not the volume. "Why isn't she along for your vacation?"

He drew in a deep breath and let it out before answering. "Because she died."

8

As she stared at the door between her and Sam, guilt knotted in Kinsey's belly. She should have kept her big mouth shut.

The man had obviously loved his fiancée. If he hadn't, he wouldn't still be so touchy. And stupid Kinsey had stirred up all those painful memories.

She squared her shoulders. As a paid companion, she should make his life happier and help him see there was still a lot to be grateful for.

While he was in the bathroom, Kinsey bypassed her suitcase full of clothes and dug into the bags from their shopping trip. She grabbed the bikini she'd purchased and quickly dressed in it, covering up with a pair of shorts and a Santorini T-shirt. She topped it off with the floppy hat Sam insisted she needed and the sunglasses he'd picked out. Then she pulled the beach bag from her suitcase, filled it with sunscreen, her mask, snorkel and the beach towels they'd purchased in the dive shop.

The bathroom door opened, and Sam stepped out, wearing a pair of black swim trunks and a gray T-shirt. He'd shaved the shadow of stubble from his chin, combed back his hair and looked so handsome Kinsey's breath caught.

He stared across the room, his blue eyes darker than usual. "I'm sorry I was so short with you."

She laughed nervously. "No. Don't be. I shouldn't have pushed. Your past is none of my business, and I had no right to dig into it." With all the courage she could muster, she pasted a broad smile on her face. "But your two weeks of vacation is my business, and I plan on making it the best two weeks of your life. So get ready for some fun. Because we're going to have it." She lifted her chin, grabbed the beach bag and headed for the door. "Do you want me to ask Mrs. D if she has sandwich fixings?"

"No. That won't be necessary." He slipped into sandals then settled sunglasses over his eyes and a white baseball cap on his head. "We can stop at a bakery or deli and grab bread and cheese."

"Sounds good." She opened the door. "Don't forget your camera. We have some photo memories to make for your commander."

She didn't wait for him to respond, setting off with a light step and a carefree attitude. Her father had always told her the best way to a happy life when you weren't feeling very happy was to fake it until you felt it. So she faked it. Pushing all the horrors of the past week behind her, she set out to have a good day with her handsome employer. And if she could manage to make him happy in the process, she would have accomplished something. Plus, she'd be one step closer to earning that plane ticket back to the States.

The path to the ocean was a maze of twists and turns and steps leading past the white buildings. Occasionally, they'd break out of the walls long enough to see the views Santorini was known for. At one point, they spotted a blue-domed church.

"Some time in the next two weeks, we need to take a taxi to Oia to see more of the beautiful blue-domed churches this island is famous for," Kinsey remarked. "They would make great backdrops for pictures to send to your commander. Not to mention great memories of your time spent here."

Sam nodded.

He hadn't spoken much since they'd left the room, but that didn't deter Kinsey. She kept up her end of the conversation and his, as well. Her goal was to get him to smile by the end of the day, if not sooner.

Though they walked in broad daylight, Kinsey was careful passing through shadowy areas, always looking for bad guys lurking there. After the attack the previous evening, she wasn't taking any chances.

Once they arrived at the main road, they caught a taxi to the beach on the east side of the island.

Kinsey ducked into a shop carrying beach gear and talked Sam into buying a mask and snorkel for himself. When they arrived at the beach, she felt a little safer.

The location had no shadows, no bad guys, and plenty of bright sunshine to cheer her day.

She spread the beach towels on the sand, stripped out of her shorts and T-shirt and squirted a liberal portion of sunscreen on her hand. "Come on, you can't go in the water all dressed like that. And you don't want to burn that beautiful skin." She winked and waited for Sam to remove his shirt, hat and sunglasses. "Turn around."

He did as she commanded.

Kinsey spread sunscreen across his massive shoulders and down his back, trying hard not to get excited by merely touching him. She kept telling herself this activity was just part of a job. As his companion and his fake fiancée, she would be expected to see to his safety and happiness. "We can't have you getting a third-degree sunburn while here. This should help."

Her hands smoothed over the hard plains and down to his narrowing waist to the edge of the elastic band on his swim trunks. By then she was barely breathing, her pulse pounding so hard she felt lightheaded.

"Done back there?"

She wished she wasn't, but she couldn't continue without making a fool of herself. "Yes," she squeaked, cleared her throat and tried again. "Yes. You can get the front."

When he turned she slapped the tube in his hand and spun away, her cheeks burning. Wow, the man had no idea how attractive he was. But Kinsey was fully aware and suffering the effects of touching him all over the hard muscles of his back.

She stared out at the water, coaching herself on how to breathe normally when big hands descended on her back. Kinsey jumped.

"Sorry. I thought you'd want me to do your back, since you were so good to do mine."

Cheeks burning, she babbled, "Yes. Yes, of course." She stood in front of him, holding her body stiff, fighting against letting the feel of his hands on her skin make her any more turned on than she already was.

The man had lost the woman he loved, for heaven's sake. He wasn't interested in her for anything other than a paid employee to help him fool his boss into thinking he was relaxing in paradise and getting his life back together.

Sweet heaven. His touch felt so good against her skin. Kinsey moaned then cringed as soon as the sound escaped her throat.

He immediately lifted his hands off her skin. "Am I being too rough?"

"Oh, no. Not at all. Maybe a little too good at it, though." She laughed shakily, stepped away, took the tube from his hands and squirted more of the lotion into her palm. "I can manage the rest. Why don't you adjust the strap on your mask and snorkel?"

"Right." But Sam didn't turn away. He continued to watch as she smeared sunscreen on her chest, arms, legs and thighs.

The sun had nothing on the heat burning inside Kinsey by the time she finished.

Sam must have realized he was staring, because he

finally turned away and pulled the snorkel and mask out of its wrapper and adjusted it to fit on his face.

Kinsey slipped her mask over her head and settled it over her eyes. "Ready?"

He nodded. "I'm ready."

"Good, because the last one in is a rotten egg." Kinsey shoved the snorkel into her mouth and took off, laughing as she plowed into the water and dove beneath the surface.

The water surged as Sam dove in beside her. For the next hour, they swam, hugging the shoreline, and discovering the sea life beneath the surface. Brightly shining fish, eels and stingrays were in abundance and just as curious about them.

By the time Kinsey climbed out of the surf, she was tired and amazed that during that entire time, she hadn't given her near-abduction a single thought.

Sam pulled off his mask and took her hand as they slogged through the waves to the shore, their feet shifting in the ebb and flow of water and sand.

When they made it back to the towels, Kinsey dropped down and stretched out, blissfully tired and ready to soak up the sunshine and the salty sea breeze.

Sam stood above her, his hands on his hips, looking around.

Kinsey patted the towel beside her. "Have a seat, and where's your camera?"

"Huh?" He glanced down.

Shading her eyes with one hand, she waved toward the beach bag. "Your camera. Now would be a good time to shoot some pictures of you having a fun at the beach." Again, she patted the towel beside her. "Sit."

He hesitated.

She laughed. "You really don't know how to relax, do you?" Kinsey sat up. "Come on. The first step is to admit you have a problem. The second is to take the pictures you need to convince your boss you're having fun and the third is to let me massage your muscles." She tipped her head. "Come on, you can do it."

Finally, he sat on the towel and pulled out his smart-phone. "My camera is in my phone." He unlocked the screen and handed it to her.

She touched the camera icon and aimed the lens at him. "Smile."

He frowned.

"Seriously. If you want your commander to think you're having a good time, you have to do better than that." She scooted over to kneel beside him on his towel and reversed the camera so that she could take a picture of them together. "Now, smile like you're having a good time." Kinsey held the phone at arm's length and grinned.

Still, Sam frowned at the phone. "A smile feels so fake."

"Fake it until you feel it, baby," she said. "That's what my dad always said."

Sam laughed.

Kinsey snapped a picture when he wasn't aware of her doing it. "That's right. When I was scared by a nightmare, he would sit at my bedside and tell me to be brave. But I was having a hard time being brave. That's when he said, fake it until you feel it."

Kinsey gave her best Wonder Woman impression, flexing her muscles. "I'd pretend I was a superhero and totally capable of anything. By the time I went to sleep I was convinced I was badass, and none of those nightmare creatures could hurt me."

"I think I would have liked your father." He touched her cheek. "He gave you such a good outlook on life."

Kinsey still held the phone, snapping pictures, though she wasn't sure what she was taking. The touch of Sam's fingers on her cheek had her heart beating fast and her breathing coming in short ragged breaths. The man didn't have to do much to turn her inside out.

All she wanted was to lean her cheek into his palm and tell him he could have her. There on the beach. In front of God and everyone.

When she realized what she was thinking, heat suffused her neck and rose all the way up her face and to the tips of her ears. She ducked away and rolled back onto her towel.

"I think we have enough pictures. I'll go through them and find the best ones for you to share with your colonel." She kept her head down, looking through the images without actually seeing them.

Meanwhile, Sam stretched out on the towel, lying on his stomach. "You're right. I don't know how to relax. It's been so long since I did absolutely nothing. Even when I have downtime in the war zones, I'm working with the mechanics on my bird or at the gym, trying to stay in shape. I don't just sit and read a book or watch videos."

"See? Your boss might have a good point." The heat in her face dissipating, Kinsey finally glanced over toward Sam. He was looking away, giving her all the time she could want to study his body from head to toe. And what a body he had! All lean and muscular. Even tanned in all the right places. "How do you stay tanned in a war zone?" Kinsey squirted some sunscreen into her palm and moved her towel over closer to his.

"I jog in shorts and sometimes get away with losing the shirt. But don't tell my commander. He'd have me up for attempted destruction of government property. So, am I getting that massage, or were you just kidding?"

She chuckled. "I'm getting there. Don't be such a grump." Kinsey ran her hands across his shoulders. "All I have is sunscreen, but I'm sure our snorkeling washed off what we applied earlier."

"So, you're killing two birds with one stone. Or one tube of lotion." He flexed his muscles beneath her fingertips.

Her heart beat with a little flare of excitement. Kinsey massaged the tight muscles around his neck, working her fingers into them to loosen the knots. "Are you always this tense?"

"I guess, for the most part. But what you're doing is amazing. It's getting me so relaxed, I could fall asleep."

"Then do it. You were up late last night rescuing me." Kinsey moved her hands lower, marveling at the breadth of the man's shoulders and the hard muscles beneath his smooth skin. What would it be like to have a man like this making love to her? Her ex had been long and lean, but not nearly as muscular.

Sam was all man, each muscle clearly defined and toned. She squirted more lotion on her hands and rubbed it into his lower back, daring to slide ever closer to the waistband of his swim trunks, wishing she had the nerve to smooth over the rounded curve of his ass.

Sweet Jesus! What was she thinking? Back up to his neck she moved, out of temptation and away from her naughty thoughts.

"Mmm. That felt good." Sam sat up and took the lotion tube from her hand. "Now, my turn."

Kinsey's face burned, and she stammered. "I don't need you to do that. Really."

"I can't have my companion getting lobstered by the sun. What good would you be to me if you're in pain or out of commission due to extreme sunburn?" He nodded toward her towel. "Assume the position."

"What?" Her pulse pounded so loudly against her eardrums she couldn't hear herself think. Which was probably why she rolled onto her stomach, against her better judgment.

Sam straddled her hips, pinning her beneath him.

Even if she wanted to get away—which she didn't— she couldn't do it easily or gracefully. With Sam perched over her, all kinds of naughty scenarios raced through her consciousness. But when he rubbed his lotion-covered hands over her shoulders, her thoughts scrambled, and she forgot how to breathe.

He leaned over her and whispered in her ear, "Are you always this tense?"

Sweet heaven. Only when she had a hot guy touching her like he was. She mumbled something. What, she didn't know.

Sam chuckled and leaned over her again. "Now, you know what you were doing to me."

"You? I thought you were falling sleep?"

"Not hardly. How can a guy sleep when he has a beautiful woman rubbing her hands over his body?"

Cheeks burning again, Kinsey forced a chuckle. "All in the name of companionship. Right?" So the words were somewhat choked out. She was determined to keep their relationship light. The man wasn't interested in her as anything other than a paid companion. Hell, he didn't want any woman on a long-term basis. He'd lost his one true love and probably had no intention of falling in love again.

What a shame. The man would sire beautiful babies, if he only let himself. Kinsey found herself wishing she could be the lucky winner of his DNA lottery. She'd carry his baby, happily.

All those insane musings ran through her head, along with fairy tales of happily ever after with the handsome helicopter pilot. But fairy tales rarely came true, her parents being the exception. The divorce statistics were proof of that. Besides, Sam was very clear he didn't want women falling all over themselves to be with him. He wanted to learn how to relax and enjoy his vacation, stress free.

Then, he unclipped her bikini bra.

Kinsey sank into the towel, afraid to rise for fear of exposing her breasts to all the people on the beach. "What are you doing?"

"Don't worry, I'll hook it back when I'm done. I didn't want to ruin the fabric with the lotion."

"Oh." What else could she say? He'd just sent her to an even deeper level of fantasy she had no hope of swimming out of while he had his hands on her naked back.

Those rough but gentle fingers worked lower and lower still to the elastic band of her bikini bottoms. Wow, if only they were alone and she wasn't working for him, she'd let him go even lower.

Sam shifted off her hips. "That should do it," he said, his voice gruff.

Kinsey grabbed her bikini bra with both hands and sat up. "I'm hungry, how about you?"

"Just like that?" He laughed. "One minute you're putty in my hands and the next you're starving?"

"That's me. My stomach rules me." She struggled to hold the bra in place while reaching behind her to reconnect the fasteners.

He moved her fingers aside. "Let me." And he secured the hooks. "Better?"

"Much." Kinsey pulled her T-shirt over her head and down her body, covering the exposed skin that quivered whenever he looked at her, much less touched her. How could she work for this man for the next two weeks when all she wanted was to beg him to make love to her? "Food. We need to find something to eat."

Sam chuckled, but he stood and shook the sand out of the towels.

Kinsey packed them away in the beach bag while Sam pulled on his shirt.

By the time they'd crossed the beach and slipped into their sandals, Kinsey's pulse had returned to normal.

"You know, the more I think about the hotel and the guys who tried to abduct you, the more I think we should go to the local police and report what happened," Sam said.

Kinsey shook her head. "I thought of that too, but I'm still waiting for my passport. I don't know what would happen if I showed up at the police station and couldn't provide proof of my citizenship."

"You have a point. But I hate to think they have some kind of human trafficking ring set up and are taking advantage of vulnerable women."

Kinsey's heart warmed. Being with Sam made her feel protected. "When I get my passport in my hot little hands, I'll be first in line at the police station. Believe me."

Sam glanced both ways and started to cross the street.

A vehicle sped out of a side road and raced toward him.

Though she saw a blur out of the corner of her eye, Kinsey barely had time to react. She grabbed his hand and yanked him out of the street, just in time.

The car sped past, rolling over the very spot Sam had been standing moments before.

Sam pulled her into his arms where she clung to him, her heart racing.

"What the hell?" Sam's jaw was tight, his eyes narrowed as he stared after the speeding car. "I swear he looked like he was aiming for me."

"No kidding. What was he thinking?" Still leaning into the strength of Sam's body, Kinsey turned her head to watch as the car disappeared around a curve in the road. "You weren't walking on his side of the road. He swerved toward you."

Sam's arms tightened around her. "Come on, let's get out of the open."

"Why would someone want to run you over?" Then a possible reason dawned on her. "Do you think he did it to get you out of the way?"

"Yeah. And I'm not happy about that fact," Sam said.

"I'm so sorry." Kinsey wrapped her arm around his waist and squeezed. "That attack was all my fault."

He pushed her to arm's length. "What are you talking about? You are not to blame."

She looked up at him, her chest tight, guilt weighing heavily on her. "But if you hadn't happened on those two men making off with me, you wouldn't have been nearly run over by that car."

He smiled gently at her. "Oh, sweetheart. Hold that thought a moment. We need to get out of the street before another car tries to make speedbumps out of us." He hurried her across the street and out of any path a car could possibly take before he stopped and pulled her into his arms. "You aren't the trouble here. You're the potential victim."

She leaned into him, smelling the fresh scent of salt on his skin. Kinsey loved the way his strength infused her body. "Now, so are you."

"I can handle the heat."

"You're supposed to be relaxing, not dodging murderous drivers."

"I am relaxing."

She laughed. "How can you, with me around?" Kinsey's smile faded and she pulled away. "I need to leave you alone. You don't deserve to be harassed because of me."

He frowned. "Are you backing out of our deal?"

"I don't see any other way to keep you safe." She took another step away.

"We have a deal. I bought your ticket home." He reached for her hand. "You owe me two weeks of companionship. A verbal contract is as binding as a written one. We shook on it."

Couldn't he see that she had to leave? To protect him? "You're in danger because of me."

His lips pressed into a thin line. "We have a binding contract. I haven't released you from it. You owe me two weeks."

Kinsey stared into his eyes. The man could have been carved in stone. He wasn't backing down or releasing her from their contract. "I think you're making a mistake."

"Yeah, but the mistake is mine to make. Now, are we good? Because I'm not relaxing by arguing with you."

"I'm sorry." Her lips quirked upward on the corners. "I'll try harder. But you don't have to be such a hard ass."

"It's the only ass I have." He chuckled. "Now, let's find some food before another car tries to run us over." He took her hand in his and weaved through the buildings until they came to a bakery with fresh bread and then stopped at another store selling cheese and olives.

Sam purchased enough food to make a decent lunch, and they took it back to the B&B, climbed the ladder to the roof and had a picnic while looking out at the amazing view.

If not for the attacks on herself and Sam, Kinsey could almost believe they were on an ideal vacation or a date.

But ideal wasn't quite the right word to describe what had happened in the past twenty-four hours. She hoped and prayed the next twenty-four were spent happily getting to know each other better and not nearly as dangerous or hair-raising.

9

SAM COULDN'T BELIEVE he'd lived through some of the most dangerous firefights a helicopter pilot could imagine, only to come to Santorini on vacation to nearly be killed by a crazed driver. That incident was something he would not be reporting to his commander.

And, since he was thinking about his report, he figured he might as well make it.

"Did you decide on a photo to share with the CO?" He pulled his phone from his pocket and handed it over to Kinsey.

She scrolled through the shots she'd taken and showed him one of himself frowning. "In this one, you're not grimacing as much as some of the others."

"No. But I look like I ate something that tasted bad." Did he always have that scowl on his face? No wonder his commander was concerned about his mental stability. "I frown too much."

"Not always, but most of the time." Kinsey laughed.

"Don't worry, by the end of these two weeks, I'll have you smiling most of the time, not frowning." She scrolled past several shots of them together.

"Wait. What about them?" He brushed his finger over the screen to back up to one of him and her. "I'm almost smiling in this one. That ought to make the old man happy." He punched the numbers to Facetime his commander and waited for the connection to go through and for his boss to answer.

Kinsey's lips curled upward. "I like that photo. You do appear almost happy there." She looked up at him. "You really should smile more. Life is too short to be unhappy all the time."

Her smile made his heart lighter than it had been in years and gave him the uncontrollable urge to... He leaned forward and kissed the tip of her nose. "Thank you for helping me with this little project."

She blinked, her smile slipping slightly as color suffused her cheeks.

Now he'd gone and done it. "Hey, I'm sorry. I crossed the line." He raised a hand. "I promise not to kiss you again...unless you ask."

Her cheeks reddened even more, and she turned away. "No. No. That's okay. I kind of liked it."

He tipped up her face toward his. "Then why are you turning so red?"

"I don't know." She shrugged. "I guess because we just met yesterday, and I shouldn't be feeling this way about you so soon."

"Feeling what way?"

"Nervous...excited... confused." She glanced up at him.

Her brow pinched in that cute way he'd come to recognize when she was hesitant or anxious. "I don't mean to make you nervous. I promise, I won't attack you like those men did."

She laughed. "I know you won't. That's what I like about you. I feel like I can trust you. After all, you've saved my life."

"And you saved mine, today." He cupped her cheek in his palm and brushed his thumb across her lips. "You had a breadcrumb." And then he stared at those lips, wishing he had kissed them instead of the tip of her nose.

"If I asked you to kiss me, would you?" she whispered.

He didn't respond with words. Instead, he lowered his head and swept his lips across hers in a light, non-threatening touch. And restraint was hard, when he wanted to kiss her and taste her.

When her hands reached up and wrapped behind his head, he gave in to his desire. The phone slipped from his hand, and he gathered Kinsey in his arms, crushing her mouth with his. And she tasted like heaven, so sweet, warm and wet—

"Captain Magnus! Hey, Sam! Yoohoo! Hello! Quit sucking face long enough to report in. That's an order!"

The sound of a man's voice broke through the well of lust Sam had fallen into. He lifted his head, a frown pulling at his brow.

"Someone's yelling at you," Kinsey whispered.

That's when Sam remembered he'd dialed Colonel Cooley. "Fuck." He grabbed for the phone and stared down at the man in desert camouflage uniform, laughing up at him. "Sir, I'm sorry. I must have dropped the phone."

His commander grinned, and he laughed out loud. "I see you finally embraced the idea of vacationing. Good to see you lose that perpetual scowl."

There it was again. Since when had he become a frowning grump?

He scrambled for something to say, his world off kilter after that kiss. "Sir, just following orders." That kiss. Holy hell, he'd completely lost himself and all sense of time and space. He glanced across at Kinsey.

The color was high in her cheeks, and her lips were slightly swollen. And they were so kissable, he wanted to do it all over again.

"Hey, focus here, Captain."

The colonel's voice brought Sam back to earth.

"I want to meet your lady friend," Colonel Cooley said.

Sam leaned close to Kinsey and held up the phone so that his commander could see both of their faces. "Sir, this is my friend, Kinsey. Kinsey, meet Colonel Cooley."

Kinsey laughed. "Nice to meet you, Sir. Sam's talked a lot about you."

The man laughed. "All bad, I'm sure."

She blushed. "Not all bad. Just that you were concerned."

The colonel nodded. "Sam's a good guy, and a helluva pilot. He just needs to lighten up."

"That's what he said." She smiled up at Sam. "I'm seeing to it that he does."

"Thank God. Someone needed to. He can't seem to pull himself out of the dark cloud he's been carrying around since he deployed." The colonel turned his head and nodded. "Coming." He faced the viewer again. "Got a job to do. Damned Taliban never knows when to quit. Out here."

"Magnus out." Sam's hand tightened on the phone as he pressed the end call button. "I should be there."

"But you're not." Kinsey took the phone from his hand and laid it on the blanket. "You heard your commander. You're supposed to be lightening up."

"How can I when my unit is fighting over there?" He drew in a deep breath and let it out slowly. "What if something happens to one of the guys while I'm not there?" He'd had the same conflicting sense of duty, as he sat with Leigha through her illness. He felt he should have been with his unit, saving the lives of so many. But he knew his duty was also to Leigha. In the end, he hadn't been able to save Leigha.

"You're not responsible for them. You have to take care of yourself." Kinsey reminded him.

"But what if I could have helped?"

Kinsey knelt behind Sam and rubbed his shoulders. "You can't think about all the bad things that could happen. My father called that borrowing trouble. You don't know what will happen. Don't always jump to the worst scenario."

"That feels good." He dropped his head forward, giving her better access to the stiff muscles in his neck.

"I know shouldn't worry about what *might* happen. But it's hard not to. I've seen too many of my buddies and the soldiers, Marines and SEALs we deliver to the hot spots come back in body bags."

"You're not there." Her fingers pressed harder. "You can't affect the outcome from here."

"Exactly. I'm not there, and I should be."

"Wow." Kinsey rubbed his neck, digging in with her soft, but firm fingers. "You're all knotted up." She patted his back and rose to her feet, pulling him up along with her. "Come on. We have to do something to keep your mind off the war and on a more calming activity."

She gathered the remaining food and stuffed it into the bag, then folded the blanket they'd been sitting on.

Sam flung the blanket over his shoulder and hooked the bag over his arm then started down the ladder. When he was down, he dropped the bag and blanket and waited at the bottom while Kinsey descended.

On the last rung, she slipped and stumbled backward.

Sam caught her in his arms and held her tight, his cheek pressed to the side of her hair. "Steady now."

"I don't know why I'm so clumsy." Kinsey laughed and turned in his arms. "But thank you." She stretched up on her toes and pressed a kiss to his lips. "Thank you for catching me."

His arms tightened around her, and he kissed her back.

Kinsey melted against him, her body fitting perfectly against his—all soft, warm, and inviting him to do so much more than kiss her.

He traced his tongue across the seam of her lips. When she opened to him, he darted in, caressing her in a long, slow glide. She tasted of cheese and fresh bread and fresh air and sunshine. He could kiss her all day long and never need another breath.

"There you are," a voice said behind him, jerking him out of that special place he went when holding Kinsey.

He turned to find Mrs. D standing in the tiny courtyard with a paper in her hand. "I thought you might want this."

Sam took the sheet and realized it was the flight reservation confirmation for Kinsey's trip to Virginia. That brought him back to earth with a thud, reminding him that anything he started in Santorini would end in Santorini. "Thank you, Mrs. D." He handed the paper to Kinsey. "I forgot I'd left it on the printer." Or had he wanted to forget it?

"Mrs. Demopolis." Kinsey touched the woman's arm. "Do you know of any festivals or activities we can attend today or later this evening? We're looking for something to do that is part of the island culture, if possible."

"Hmm." Mrs. D touched a finger to her chin and squinted toward a corner of the building. Then her eyes widened and she smiled. "Yes. A festival is happening this evening in Oia near the blue-domed churches."

"Could we get a taxi to take us there?" Kinsey asked.

"I have a car," she announced with a nod. "You may borrow it."

"Thank you, but we don't want to inconvenience you," Sam said.

"No inconvenience. I rarely use it." She waved toward them. "Please, take it. I won't need it today."

"Thank you, Mrs. Demopolis." Kinsey kissed the woman's cheek, making the landlady blush.

"Please, I am Esma. Call me Esma."

"Thank you, Esma."

And like that, Kinsey had the landlady in love with her. Sam stood back and shook his head, a smile turning up the corners of his mouth. How did she do that? She'd been through so much, and yet, she kept on smiling.

He needed a woman like this to keep him from taking life so seriously. He needed Kinsey.

And the thought scared him to death.

AFTER A QUICK SHOWER TO rinse out the salt from her hair and off her skin, Kinsey pulled a sundress over her head and smoothed it down her body. She combed the tangles from her hair and pulled the damp tresses into a ponytail at the nape of her neck.

When she stepped out of the bathroom, Sam hurried inside. "Five minutes, and I'll be ready."

"I'll let you have ten. That's what I took."

"Five. Start counting." He closed the door, and the shower started immediately.

Kinsey stared at the door, wishing she had the nerve to have shared her shower. They could have gotten done so much faster.

Or not.

Her core heated, and her blood flowed like molten lava through her veins. If they'd shared a shower, she would have said to hell with the festival and stayed in the bathroom until the water turned cold. And then she'd have dried him off from head to toe, exploring every inch of his naked body.

She touched her fingers to her still-swollen lips. His kisses had been nothing like anything she'd ever shared with her ex. Where Travis's were lukewarm, Sam's were hot, hot, hot!

All the nerves in her body had come alive as if they'd been jump-started with a jolt of electricity big enough to light up all of Santorini.

Her shower had been cool enough it should have chilled the heat burning through her body. But it hadn't. Now, as she stood staring at the bathroom door, all she could think of was that Sam was naked on the other side.

Kinsey pressed her hands to her heated cheeks. Sweet heaven, what was she going to do? Was she falling in love with the man? Lust, yeah. That for sure. But the feeling was more than that.

Sam was a military pilot, risking his life every time he flew a mission. Hero material.

How could she let herself fall in love—if, in fact, that was what she was feeling? She knew the stakes. The man was not committing to anything. Kinsey was heading back to Virginia at the end of her stay on Santorini. They'd never see each other again. Hell, she didn't even know where he was stationed when he was Stateside. Not that his location mattered. Again, he wasn't into commitment.

Kinsey squared her shoulders. She'd known what

she was getting into when she shook on the deal. Now wasn't the time to get cold feet or have regrets.

Why should she regret spending time with a handsome man, exploring this beautiful Greek island? So she wouldn't see him after they parted ways. She'd have some great memories to tide her over for a long time. With that silent pep talk, she was ready to face anything.

And then Sam stepped out of the bathroom, dressed in khaki slacks and a white polo shirt. The contrast with his pitch-black hair and light blue eyes made him so breathtakingly handsome, Kinsey forgot how to breathe.

"Are you ready?" he asked.

Unable to push non-existent air past her vocal cords, she nodded.

"You might want to wear shoes." He chuckled,

The sound spread over her like melted caramel. Heat burned her cheeks, and she ducked low to hide her face and find the sandals he'd purchased earlier that day. All the while, she scolded herself.

Get a grip, girl.

He's not in the market for a relationship.

Don't drool.

She fumbled with the buckle on her sandal, her hands shaking.

"Here, let me." Before she could utter a protest, Sam knelt beside her and buckled the thin strap of her sandal, his fingers brushing against her ankle sent electric currents all the way through her body and directly to her core.

He adjusted the other one while she forced air in and

out of her lungs. When he was done, he rose, held out his hand and helped her to her feet. "You're beautiful."

"So are you," she blurted. Her face burned and she turned away, spotted his phone on an end table and grabbed it. "Let's do a photo for the boss." She held it at arm's length. "Come on, get in the picture."

He closed the distance between them, wrapped an arm around her shoulders and smiled at the screen. Then he frowned. "What's wrong?"

"What? Why do you ask?"

"You're not smiling."

Kinsey looked at her reflection in the phone's screen and realized he was right. She pasted a smile on her face to rectify the oversight and clicked the button. "I'll let you send that while I apply some lipstick." She dove for the bathroom and shut the door.

She hadn't applied much makeup and was glad. What she needed was to step back into a cold shower for an hour to bring her body temperature back to normal. Instead, she wet a washcloth, squeezed out the excess moisture and pressed it to her fevered brow.

This job might be one of the hardest assignments she'd ever had. Especially if he kissed her again.

She stared at her reflection in the mirror and reminded herself that Sam had said he wouldn't kiss her unless she asked him. And she'd asked. The way to solve her problem was to keep her mouth shut and not ask for any more of those soul-defining kisses that rocked her world and made her forget an end would eventually come to anything between the two of them.

When the color in her cheeks finally retreated to a

soft pink, she took a deep breath and stepped out of the bathroom with a smile on her face. "I'm ready."

He looked at her with a quizzical expression. "I thought you were going to apply lipstick?"

Damn. The heat started back into her cheeks, but she wouldn't hide in the bathroom again. "I changed my mind." She flipped her ponytail and winked. "It's a woman's prerogative to change her mind. Didn't you know that?"

He laughed, hooked her arm and guided her toward the door. "Then we'd better go, before you change your mind about this festival."

God help her. When Sam smiled, the whole world was brighter. Or was it the sunshine on Santorini that made her happier?

She refused to dig deeper for the underlying reason for the spring in her step. She'd learned a long time ago to live in the moment and be happy for gift of today.

Why not let that be her motto regarding Sam? Be happy with him now. She didn't have to borrow sadness from tomorrow.

And if she wanted another kiss today, she'd by golly ask for it.

Her heart might be in big trouble two weeks from that moment, but not on this day with Sam.

10

SAM WISHED he'd hired a taxi for their trip to Oia. Though the journey wasn't that far, considering Santorini wasn't a big island, the tiny interior of the smart car made the trip seem longer.

He'd had to fold himself into the driver's seat and sit with his knees up to his chin. Mrs. D was at least a foot shorter than he was. A smart car made sense for the woman. And she'd been so happy to loan it to them, that he hadn't had the heart to turn down her kind offer.

"You know, I could drive."

"I'd be just as cramped in the passenger seat," Sam said. "I can do this is if you help me make sure I'm in the right gear, since I can't see the gear shift past my leg." He glanced at her. "You know how to drive a five speed?"

She grinned. "My father taught me on his pride and joy, a '67 Mustang convertible he restored."

"Nice car," Sam said. "That model had a lot more leg room."

She laughed. "My dad loved that car. He'd take it to the antique car shows and prop open the hood. He kept the engine clean enough to eat off."

"Your dad sounds like he would have been pretty special."

"He was." She sighed. "He always got my mother chocolates and flowers on Valentine's Day, even when he wasn't at home. He made sure someone delivered them. And he never forgot their anniversary."

"The man was a saint." Sam drove along the coast, headed toward the tip of the island.

"What about your family?" Kinsey asked. "Are your parents still around?"

"Oh, yeah. They're on a cruise right now. We just left Ireland a few days ago where my brother, Wyatt, got married."

"You're so very lucky." Kinsey smiled. "I always wanted a brother."

"My father wanted more children, but Mom put down her foot when Dad wanted to keep trying for a girl."

"How wonderful for you to grow up with all those siblings."

Sam slowed for a car turning onto the road ahead of him. "We fought a lot, but all four of us would take a bullet for the rest."

Kinsey stared out the windshield. "If I ever have children, I want at least four. I'd never have only one."

He chuckled. "What if you could only have one?"

"Then I'd adopt the other three. I never want a child of mine to grow up alone."

"Was it hard being an only child?" Sam asked. "I can imagine it would have been a lot easier not having to fight for space in the bathroom or share a room with someone else."

"Yeah, there is that, but life as an only child can be lonely. I always wished I had siblings. I dreamed about being a big sister or the aunt to my nieces and nephews. Who knows, I might still have a shot at the aunt role, but only if I'm lucky enough to marry a man with siblings."

Sam had enough brothers to share. His stomach fluttered at the thought he had the qualifications to be a potential husband to Kinsey. What would it be like to be married to a woman like her? Would his brothers accept her as part of the Magnus clan? Why was he thinking along those lines? He wasn't in the market to marry. "What about your extended family? Do you have any aunts or uncles?" Sam asked.

She snorted. "My parents were only children. That fact was one of the reasons they were attracted to each other. They understood what the situation was like."

"Why didn't they have more children?"

"They tried, but it just didn't happen." Kinsey stared out the window at the coastline. "I came along later in their lives. Surprising them when they thought they were done. I was their only shot at being parents. And they were the best."

Sam glanced across at Kinsey.

She was smiling.

He liked the way she talked about her parents, how much she loved them and wanted to be like them. He felt the same. His family meant the world to him. Growing up with his brothers had been one adventure after another. He knew how fortunate he was to still have both his parents.

Kinsey talked of growing up in Virginia, and Sam shared some of the crazy stunts he and his brothers pulled as kids and teens in Texas.

Soon, they were pulling into the town of Oia on the northern tip of the island. Like Imerovigli, whitewashed structures clung to the hillsides. Sam parked the car near the shore, helped Kinsey out and locked the door. Using the directions Mrs. D had kindly provided, they climbed to the blue-domed churches where vendors had set up tents and booths with food, crafts and clothing for sale. In an open area, a band played lively music.

The sun was on its daily slide into the ocean, making for another spectacular view.

Sam stood with his arm around Kinsey and let the colors wash over him, seeming to cleanse the worry from his mind.

Being with Kinsey made him realize how much of life and laughter he'd been missing. She showed him an entirely different outlook and how to embrace the good each day brought. The woman made him feel lighter and happier than he'd felt in years.

The music rose in volume as the sun disappeared. Twinkle lights lit the square where people danced and laughed.

When the band segued into a flowing waltz, Sam asked Kinsey, "Do you want to dance?"

She listened to the music and her brow wrinkled. "I don't know. It's been a long time since I danced a waltz." She looked up at him. "Do you even know how to waltz?"

He looked down his nose and gave her his most offended look. "Madame, I'll have you know I'm an excellent waltzer. Or whatever you call it."

Kinsey's eyebrows rose up her forehead. "I'm having a hard time imagining that."

"Then quit imagining and let me demonstrate." He held out his hand.

When she laid her fingers against his palm, he spun her out and back into his arms, holding her in the proper frame for a waltz. Then he led her into the square where a few older couples were waltzing and proceeded to show her just how good he could be.

Kinsey laughed and followed each of his steps. "You are an amazing dancer. Who taught you?"

He dipped his head. "Thank you. My mother will be happy to know all those years of forcing us to learn paid off. She said the way to a man's heart was through his stomach. But the way to a woman's heart was talent on the dance floor."

"Your mother is brilliant."

His heart swelled with pride. "I'll let her know you said so. Who taught you to waltz?'

"I mentioned my parents were older, right? Well, call them old-fashioned, but they took ballroom dance together and had me enrolled at a very young age. I was waltzing when I was four."

Sam grinned, remembering the photo she'd shown him of the young Kinsey. He could imagine her as a little girl in a dance class, twirling around the floor. "Now, that I can picture. I bet you were a cute little four-year-old."

She smiled and winked. "I had my choice of dance partners. All between fifty and seventy years old."

The song ended, and a lively salsa played. "Now, this tempo is where my Texas roots will come in handy," Sam said. "Ever do the salsa?"

Kinsey laughed. "No, but if you lead, I'll follow."

Sam proved that not only could he waltz, but he could salsa and two-step like a pro. By the time they left the festival after eleven o'clock, Sam was laughing and exhilarated by their lively dancing.

On the way back to the B&B, the music still played in his head, and he tapped his fingers on the steering wheel. "I don't remember the last time I went dancing. Probably in college."

"Me, too. And what a shame. It's great exercise. Between the snorkeling and the dancing, I think I dropped five pounds."

They entered the B&B and tiptoed past Mrs. D's rooms.

Sam stuck the key in the lock and started to turn it when he realized the door wasn't even closed. Alarm bells went off in his head. He tensed and pushed Kinsey behind him. "Stay back."

"Why? What's wrong?" she whispered.

"The door was open. Stay here." He gave the door a slight push.

Kinsey grabbed his arm. "What are you doing?"

"I'll check it out and let you know if it's clear."

"Are you crazy?" She hung onto his arm, preventing him from crossing the threshold. "What if someone is still in there?"

Before he could respond, the door was flung all the way open, and a man charged out, plowing into Sam. He hit him like a linebacker, going for the tackle, slamming him against the opposite wall.

Kinsey yelped and backed away.

Sam hit the wall so hard his breath was knocked from his lungs, but he refused to let it incapacitate him. He had to fight back. If he went down, that action would leave Kinsey exposed to whatever the attacker had in mind. And Sam refused to let that happen.

KINSEY STAGGERED BACKWARD, stunned by the speed and force of the attack on Sam. She backed into a wrought iron chair that was part of a bistro table set. Her fingers curled around the chair as instinct kicked in.

The man who'd more or less tackled Sam balled his fist, cocked his arm and was about to punch Sam.

Kinsey lifted the chair and whipped it toward the attacker, catching him in the cocked arm.

The blow didn't knock out the attacker, and probably didn't hurt him that badly, but it distracted him long enough for Sam to regain his balance and come back fighting.

He swung his fist, connecting with the man's gut. As the man doubled over, Sam hit him with an upper cut to the jaw, sending him flying back against the wall.

Mrs. D flung open her door, cursing in Greek. When she saw what was happening, she squealed and ran back into her apartment, shouting something about calling the police. Or, at least, that's what Kinsey understood. She prayed the woman stayed in her apartment until the attacker was incapacitated or left.

Kinsey didn't care as long as Sam and Mrs. D were all right. With that in mind, she grabbed the chair from where it had fallen and went after the guy pushing away from the wall. He wouldn't get another chance to hurt Sam. Not if Kinsey could help it. She swung the chair as hard as she could, but he caught it, pushed it back at her then he raced for the exit.

The force with which he flung back the chair sent Kinsey stumbling backward. She slammed into the bistro table, knocking it over, and she fell to the ground.

Sam had started after the assailant, but when he saw Kinsey drop, he stopped and turned back.

She wanted to tell him not to worry about her, but she didn't want Sam to go after the bad guy. Another one could be waiting outside the building, ready to gang up on Sam.

Sam knelt beside Kinsey. "Are you okay?"

"I'm all right." When she reached for his hand, a sharp pain in her side made her wince.

"You're not all right."

"I am. It's just a bruise. I'll live." She pushed past the pain and stood, straightening her dress. "I'm more worried about you. He hit you pretty hard." She glanced at his knuckles and winced. "And look at your hand." Kinsey took his hand in hers. "Your knuckles are bleeding."

Sam's lips twisted. "Yeah. He had a jaw like a brick wall. But I got a good one in." He set Kinsey to the side. "Let me make sure no one else is in the room."

"I'm going with you," Kinsey insisted.

Sam shook his head. "Stay here." He set the chair upright and scooted it over to her. "Use this, if you have to." Before she could protest again, he entered the room.

Mrs. D opened her door a crack and peered out. "Is the man gone?"

Kinsey nodded and pressed a finger to her lips, pointed at the door to Sam's room.

Mrs. D's eyes widened, and she waved Kinsey to come inside her apartment.

Kinsey shook her head. She wasn't going anywhere without Sam. Instead, she picked up the chair and walked toward the door Sam had gone through.

As she crossed the threshold, Sam appeared in front of her.

"All clear." He pulled her into his arms.

Kinsey dropped the chair, wrapped her arms around Sam's neck and buried her face against his chest. "When that bastard ran into you so hard, I thought he'd break every bone in your body." She swept her hands over his chest and ribs. "Did he?"

Sam chuckled and winced when she touched a certain spot. "No, only bruised." He tilted back her head

---

and looked into her eyes. "I wanted to kill him when he flung the chair at you."

"Mother Mary, what happened?" Mrs. D appeared in the doorway, her eyes wide, pressing a shaking hand to her chest. "Who was that man?"

Sam and Kinsey turned to the landlady.

"We don't know." Sam crossed to the door where he pointed at the doorjamb. "He forced his way in past the lock."

The older woman ran her hand over the damaged wood. "I was listening to music. I didn't hear it. I am so sorry."

"It's not your fault."

"I will put you in another room. You cannot stay here tonight." She hurried down the hallway to another door. "You can stay in here. I will have my cousin fix the other door tomorrow." She removed a key from her keychain and handed it to Sam. "This intrusion has not happened before. I don't understand."

Kinsey didn't enlighten the woman for fear she'd ask them to leave and take the danger with them.

"Thank you, Mrs. Demopolis," Sam said. "We'll clear our things out of the other room and strip the sheets from the bed."

"No. No. I will take care of it tomorrow. The hour's late. You need your rest." She would have helped them carry their things, but Kinsey insisted they could manage.

Mrs. D reluctantly returned to her apartment, wringing her hands and promising she'd have her cousin install another lock on the main entrance. In the meantime, she'd lock the common door since they were the only guests in the B&B for the night.

Kinsey gathered her new clothes and toiletries, shoved them into her old suitcase along with all of her worldly goods and managed to close it long enough to carry it across the hall.

Sam stuffed his things into his duffel bag and slung it over his shoulder. He followed Kinsey, staying close to her.

She liked that he was there. He made her feel safe in what was beginning to feel like a very dangerous place. Apparently, whoever had attacked her the first night now knew where she stayed. The next time, she and Sam might not be as lucky to escape.

The thought made her slow as she entered the equally quaint room with similar furnishings. One chair, one queen-sized bed and a small table with two chairs. Again, the view was through a small window overlooking a courtyard.

Sam closed the door and locked it. "You can have the bed. I'll sleep on the floor."

Kinsey shook her head. "No way. This is your vacation. I'm the hired help. I'll sleep on the floor. Besides, this situation is all my fault. If you hadn't saved me, you wouldn't have men slamming into you and breaking your ribs. I really should leave and let you get on with your life."

Sam dropped his duffel bag on the floor, took her suitcase from her hand and set it down as well. Then he gathered her into his arms. "This incident is not your fault. I'm glad I found you before those guys took you away. Otherwise, I never would have gone snorkeling or dancing."

His words made her feel a little better. Perhaps she was helping him after all. She touched his shirt, her fingers curling into the soft fabric. "You could have."

"Probably not. Doing those things is not fun unless you have someone to share them with. And where would I have found a dance partner that would let me stomp on her toes?"

She laughed. "You're too good of a dancer to stomp on anyone's toes." She pressed her forehead to his chest. "I feel like I'm the one with the dark cloud following me. I'm bad luck."

"I'll take your kind of luck. I haven't had this much fun in too long to remember." He kissed her forehead. "Thank you for reminding me I have a life I need to live."

"Yeah. If you get to live it." She looked up at him. "What if that man had done more permanent damage? I could never forgive myself if he had."

"Again, what happened is not your fault. If I didn't like having you around, I might have turned over your problems to the police by now."

"So, you like me?" she asked, a tenuous smile spreading across her lips. "That's good, because I like you, too."

He bent and kissed the tip of her nose. "Sometimes, I think I like you too much." He kissed her right cheek and then aimed for the left.

The warmth of his lips and the scent of his after-shave made Kinsey's insides heat. She turned her face in time to keep him from kissing her other cheek, bringing her lips close to his. "If I ask you to, will you kiss me?"

"I wouldn't resist." He covered her mouth with his and gathered her even closer in his arms. "I couldn't."

This spot was where Kinsey wanted to be, where she felt safest. Where her world seemed to begin. She felt as if this man was who she'd been waiting for her entire life. Travis hadn't been the one for her. But being with her ex had led her to take the leap. All the bad things that had happened to her led to this one, glorious good thing.

Finding Sam.

She gave in and let the feelings and emotions wash over her. So what if their arrangement only lasted a day, a week, or two? She'd have him for now.

"If I asked you to make love to me, would you?" she whispered, leaning her breasts against his chest.

He tightened his hold on her. "Are you asking?"

Her heart pounded as she cupped his cheek in her palm and nodded. "Please, make love to me."

Sam closed his eyes, sucked in a deep breath that expanded his chest and let it out. Then he bent, scooped her into his arms and carried her to the bed.

Sam set her on her feet, raised her arms over her head and bent to gather the hem of her dress. He dragged it excruciatingly slowly up her body, his hands skimming her hips, her ribs, the swells of her breasts along the way. Then he tossed the dress over the single chair and looked down at her. "You can always say no, and I'll stop."

"Please." She trembled in anticipation. "Don't stop. I want this."

"Not as my paid companion?"

"No. As a woman. Who needs a man. Who needs you and only you." She tugged his shirt out of the waistband of his khaki slacks and dragged it up his body and over his head.

With his chest bared, she could see the definition of every sinew and the six-pack row of muscles across his abdomen. Her mouth went dry. She swept her tongue across her lips as she reached for the button on his trousers and slipped it free.

Sam circled his hands around her back and unhooked the clasp on her bra, sliding the straps over her shoulders and down her arms until the garment dropped to the floor.

Standing in front of him wearing only her panties and the sandals he'd bought for her, she shivered in anticipation.

"You are so very beautiful."

Her cheeks heated. "And you are wearing entirely too many clothes."

"We should remedy that. Right away." But he didn't make a move to discard his pants.

Taking matters into her own hands, Kinsey lowered his zipper until his cock sprang free into her palm. The man went commando.

Her pulse ricocheted off the walls of her veins and arteries, shooting blood through her to pool at her core where she ached to feel him inside and filling her so full she couldn't breathe for the ecstasy of their joining.

Too deep into her rising passion, she shucked her panties, kicked off her sandals and helped him push his pants over his hips and down his legs.

Sam toed off his shoes and stepped free of his pants and stood before her as naked as she.

If she thought he was sexy in his swim trunks, he was beyond anything she could have imagined standing there with his cock jutting out long, thick and proud.

Kinsey took his hand and drew him toward the bed, pausing before she climbed onto the mattress. "Damn."

"What's wrong?" He bent to press a kiss to the hollow at the base of her throat.

"Protection."

"Got it." He lifted his slacks from the floor, dug into his back pocket and pulled free his wallet. Inside, he had three condoms. He set them on the nightstand. Then he swept Kinsey off her feet and laid her on the bed.

"Are you always so prepared?"

"My father taught me a few lessons, as well."

"I think I'd like your father."

"I know he would like you." Sam climbed onto the bed and lay down beside her, trailing a finger from her temple to her cheek.

Kinsey took that finger and guided it lower, tracing a line down her neck and over the swell of her breasts where she pressed his palm against one.

He took the cue and cupped the orb, rolling her nipple between his thumb and forefinger and teasing the tip into a tight little bead. Then he bent to take it into his mouth where he tongued it.

Gasping, she lifted off the bed, her back arching,

offering him more. Never had she had a man make love to her like this. Sam took his time, tasting and touching her body, making her just as excited as him.

By the time he left her breasts and tongued his way across her belly to the triangle of hair across her sex, she was breathless and ready for so much more. "Please," she moaned.

"Please what?" he asked, blowing a warm stream of air across the ruffle of curls.

"I want you. Now." She laced her hands into his hair and urged him lower.

He complied, parted her folds and flicked her nubbin gently.

Kinsey writhed against the sheets, a low moan rising up her throat. "Yes. Oh, sweet heaven, yes!"

Alternating between laving and flicking her with his tongue, he sent her senses into a frenzy. Her body tensed as she rose to the peak and shot over the edge of her climax, catapulting toward the stars. She rode the wave as long as it lasted, slowly drifting back to earth.

The whole time, Sam lavished his amazing skills on her sex. When she could once again think, she dug her fingers into his scalp and urged him upward. "I need you inside me."

His gaze hungry, he climbed up her body and reached for one of the packets on the nightstand and tore it open.

Kinsey took it from him and rolled it down over his engorged staff, all the way to the base. She rolled his balls between her fingers, massaging them, liking that her touch made him even harder.

He settled his body between her legs and touched her there with the tip of his cock. "Again. You have the power. Say no and I stop here."

"Are you kidding me? I wouldn't have started this if I'd had any reservations. I want you to make love to me." She drew up her knees, gripped his ass in each of her hands and pressed him into her hard and fast.

He drove deep inside, filling every inch of her channel with his thick length, stretching her and making her fully aware of just how big he was. And she wanted all of him.

He held steady, allowing her to adjust to his length and girth.

When she was ready, she guided him back out and in, setting the rhythm by starting at a slow, steady pace.

As her core heated again, she wanted him faster, hard and deeper. She gripped his buttocks and helped to him to understand her need.

Then, she lost herself in the moment.

Sam took over, pumping in and out of her so hard and fast, they shook the white iron bed, making soft bumping sounds against the wall.

Kinsey half-laughed and half-gasped as she rose with the swell of desire to the peak and again toppled over the other side.

Sam thrust once more and stayed buried deep inside, his cock throbbing with the pulse of his release.

Eventually, Kinsey relaxed, her body spent and replete, completely satisfied for the moment. "Give me a few minutes' rest," she whispered, her eyes closing. "And I'll be ready to go again."

He laughed and pulled her over onto her side beside him without breaking their intimate connection. "You might be ready, but I think recovery time will be longer for me. You were amazing."

She chuckled. "And you thought you wouldn't enjoy Santorini." She opened her eyes and stared up into his.

"Santorini is not what is making this vacation magical." He drew her face closer and kissed her lips.

His mouth tasted of her sex, making Kinsey's body stir all over again. "If not Santorini, then what?" Travis never talked during sex. Kinsey wanted to hear the words.

"It's you, Kinsey. You make me smile. Your relentless optimism is hard to deny, and your smile rivals the Mediterranean sunshine."

She stroked his beard-stubbled chin, her heart warming to his words. "Better watch it flyboy, you're waxing poetic. What would our commander think?"

"He'd think I finally got a grip and congratulate me."

Her joy dimmed. "But I've brought more havoc than joy to your trip."

"If not for the havoc, I wouldn't know the joy. I think fate brought me to that alley and that set of steps where those men had you. I was supposed to be there to find you."

"Yeah?" She leaned closer and kissed him. "Well, maybe next time you date a girl you can meet her in a more conventional location." Not that she wanted to think of him dating anyone else. The thought took some of the happiness out of the euphoric haze she floated in from their lovemaking.

Kinsey had a little over a week and a half left with Sam. She would make it the best ten days ever. And when they parted, she wouldn't cry or make him feel bad about leaving her. She'd be happy about what little time she had with him and get on with her life.

That was her plan, and she was sticking to it. As she lay beside him, wrapped in the warmth and security of his arms, a single tear slipped from the corner of her eye and dropped onto the pillow.

So, she'd let one tear slip. She would never let him see them. He couldn't know how much he was beginning to mean to her.

11

SAM WOKE the next morning and rolled over to gather Kinsey in his arms, only to find the pillow beside him empty. His pulse leaped, and he went from groggy to instantly alert and sitting up. "Kinsey?" How could he not have heard her rising from the bed and moving around the room?

The bathroom door opened, and Kinsey came out, dressed in her bikini top and shorts. "Hey, sleepyhead. Did I wake you making too much noise?" She sat on the edge of the bed and ran her hand through his hair. "What's wrong?"

He shook his head, willing his heart to slow its rapid beating. "Nothing's wrong." Now that he knew she hadn't been kidnapped and carried away by some bastard. "Come here." He slipped his hand around her waist and drew her down on the bed. "I missed you." But he didn't kiss her. Instead, he waited.

She laughed and smiled at him. "How about I put in

146

a standing request for you to kiss me whenever you feel like it?"

"That suits me fine." Then he kissed her, his cock swelled and he remembered where they'd left off the night before.

"And that goes for making love, too," she whispered against his lips.

He had her out of her shorts, the bikini beneath and the top before she finished the sentence. Thankfully, he'd brought enough condoms for the night before and the morning after. He'd have to remember to pick up some more that day, especially since she'd just given him permission to make love anytime he liked.

And he liked making love to her in the morning light, taking his time to make sure she was satisfied before he came inside her. Then he carried her into the shower where he made love to her again, hitting all of her favorite spots and using the last of the condoms. By the time they turned off the water, they were pushing too close to Mrs. D's last call for breakfast. They dressed and ran down the hall in the nick of time.

Mrs. D was clearing the tables, carrying cutlery and plates to the kitchen when they entered the dining room, cheeks flushed and laughing.

She smiled. "I had about given up on you."

Sam hadn't felt this invigorated or full of life in such a long time. He'd gone the entire night without thinking or dreaming about flying, his unit or the war. All because of Kinsey, and her sunny outlook on a life that had been anything but kind in the past few days.

Mrs. D emerged through the swinging door of the

kitchen, carrying a tray with scrambled eggs, beans, tomatoes and various deli meats.

A big man with dark hair and bushy eyebrows followed her. He wore the uniform of the Santorini police.

Kinsey stiffened beside Sam.

Mrs. D tipped her head toward the man as she set the tray on the sideboard. "This is my cousin, Athan. He came when he heard we had a visitor last night."

Sam shook hands with the officer. "Sir."

"Please, don't let me keep you from your breakfast," Athan said, his English laced with a British accent.

Kinsey shook the man's hand, as well. "We'll sit, if you'll join us."

Athan grinned. "Esma is a brilliant cook. I cannot pass on the opportunity, as long as we discuss business."

Kinsey glanced at Sam and then smiled. "Agreed. And it would be nice if Mrs. Demopolis would join us, as well."

Mrs. D waved her hands. "I have eaten, but I haven't had my espresso." She set the dishes on the table and left to return a few minutes later with coffee for Sam, tea for Kinsey and espresso for herself and Athan.

As Sam, Kinsey and Mrs. D's cousin feasted on the breakfast provided, Athan questioned them on what had happened and what the assailant looked like.

"Why would someone break into my house?" Mrs. D asked.

Kinsey inhaled and let it out slowly.

Sam placed a hand on her leg beneath the table and gave a slight shake of his head. He didn't want her to tell the landlady anything that she wasn't ready to share. The choice was hers.

"I'm sorry, but I think it's because I'm here." And she spilled the whole story of her coming to Greece, having her money and identification stolen, then meeting with the Martins and coming to Santorini as their au pair.

Mrs. D's eyes grew rounder and Athan's lips thinned as Kinsey told what sounded like an incredible story, all the way through to what had happened at the hotel.

Sam filled in what he had encountered and Mrs. D gave her account of the night before. When they were done, silence fell on the small gathering.

Athan shook his head. "I am sorry to say we are aware of a human trafficking issue happening right here on our island. But we have not been able to pinpoint the source or capture those in charge. We have had a number of female tourists and women with temporary work visas disappear from our shores, and we have not solved a single case." Frowning, he sighed. "This news disturbs me greatly, but thank you for the lead on the hotel. As the detective on this case, I will question the staff myself."

"Find Giorgio. I think they might have let him go when the plan to nab me was thwarted," Kinsey tapped a finger on the table. "They might be erasing any evidence of my stay at the hotel to cover their asses."

Athan nodded. "I will do that. And I will look through port documents and see if I can locate when exactly the Martins left Santorini and where they were headed. I'll have my contacts in Athens be on the lookout for them. If they are luring women into service as an au pair only to have the females disappear later, they are part of the ring."

"Before I left Athens, I applied at the embassy for a replacement for my passport. I told the management at the Porto Takisi hotel to forward it to this address. It should be here any day."

Mrs. D clapped a hand to her mouth. "I'm so sorry. A package arrived for you in this morning's post." She jumped up from the table and bolted out of the dining room, returning with an envelope.

When Kinsey tore it open, she smiled and clutched her new passport to her chest. "Oh, thank God. I felt like I was without an identity when I lost my passport." Her smile spread wider. "I'm somebody now."

"You always were an amazing someone, with or without the passport." Sam squeezed her leg, sad that she'd felt so lost without the document, but glad she'd received it.

"Yeah, but having my passport makes me feel like I belong somewhere." She turned to Athan. "I lost my temporary passport when the kidnappers took me. I was afraid to report these happenings to the authorities until I received my passport. I thought the police might throw me in jail for being without identification."

Athan's lips twisted. "We would not have detained you. We are not barbarians."

"I know, but I didn't feel comfortable, being in a foreign country where I don't have a full grasp of the Greek language."

"Most of our police speak fluent English. We would

have helped." He reached across the table and touched her hand.

Sam's lips thinned and his fist clenched. He wasn't happy about another man touching Kinsey.

"Please, do not hesitate if something else happens, or you remember any more details about the men who attacked you." Athan rose from the table and thanked Mrs. D with a big hug and a promise to visit more often.

Sam and Kinsey followed Athan and Mrs. D to the exit.

Athan turned to Kinsey. "Please be safe, Miss Phillips. If these people are still after you, they might not stop until they succeed."

Kinsey nodded. "I'll be careful."

The meeting with the detective did not make Sam feel any better about what was happening to Kinsey. He slipped an arm around her waist and drew her close. "I'll be with her at all times."

"Should we move to another location, now that they know where I'm staying?" Kinsey asked. "I don't want Mrs. Demopolis to be in danger because of me."

Mrs. D threw back her shoulders. "You will stay here. Those men will not make it back into my house. I have my cousin coming to change the locks and fix the broken door. You will be safe here in the house of Demopolis." She lifted her chin and stood as tall as her five-foot-nothing frame could be.

"Thank you, Mrs. Demopolis." Kinsey hugged the older woman.

Mrs. D patted Kinsey's back. "Please, you must call me Esma."

"Thank you, Esma. You've been very kind and welcoming,"

"You two remind me of my sons and daughter. You are like family. And family takes care of each other." She touched Athan's arm. "Am I right?"

"Yes, you are, cousin." He kissed both of her cheeks and stepped through the door. "Take care."

Mrs. D watched as the man walked away and then turned to Kinsey and Sam. "I have work to do, but if you need anything, just ask."

"We're going out today to do some sailing."

Mrs. D's brows descended. "Is it safe?"

"We can't hide inside all day," Kinsey said. "We'll be fine. So far, the attacks have been primarily at night, except for the near hit-and-run. I think we'll be okay in broad daylight if we remain vigilant. Besides, Sam's here to vacation. I won't let my little issue interfere with his time off."

Mrs. D looked from Kinsey to Sam. "Please, be careful. I will be here all day if you need me." She left them in the hallway and hurried back to the dining room.

Sam took Kinsey's hand in his. "I wouldn't mind staying inside all day," he said, giving her a wicked smile.

She lifted his hand to cup her face and pressed a kiss to his palm. "We can, later today, but I've arranged for us to go sailing. That is, if you don't mind spending the money."

"We can spend the money," he assured her. "What kind of sailing did you have in mind?"

"Have you ever been sailing?" she asked, her eyes twinkling with excitement.

"Never. I grew up around San Antonio, Texas. We visited the beach at South Padre and Port Aransas, went boating, fishing and snorkeling and some scuba, but we never went sailing."

"Well, you're in for some fun today." She grinned. "I rented a small sailboat. I'm teaching you how to sail."

His brow knit. "Do you know how?"

"I do. We spent enough time on Virginia Beach during the summers that I learned how. Now you'll learn, as well." She took his hand and led him back to the room where she packed the beach bag with towels and sunscreen.

Armed with hats and sunglasses, they left the B&B and headed to the coast.

Sam made certain to guide her on a different route from the one they'd taken yesterday and remained on high alert for any movement from shadows as they passed through the alleys and up the steps to the main road. There, they caught a taxi to the beach side of the island.

As Kinsey promised, she'd reserved a small sailboat, barely big enough for both of them to sit on, but she taught him the basics in the few hours they spent in the sunshine.

Sam couldn't remember when he'd laughed so hard or had as much fun. She took pictures of him with his cellphone, and they texted them to Colonel Cooley, showing him how much he was missing.

The colonel responded with a curt, "Bastard." He

followed with, "Glad you're relaxing and having a good time. At this rate, you'll be fit to fly at the end of your two weeks."

His commander's response made Sam even happier as Kinsey splashed him with warm Mediterranean salt water and dared him to man the craft on his own. His only regret was that when the two weeks were over, he wouldn't see Kinsey again.

By the time they returned to shore, Sam was hungry. They found a small café overlooking the water, ate freshly grilled seafood and vegetables and drank wine. Then they ducked into a small store where they found snacks and, thankfully, a box of condoms. Kinsey teased him about buying an entire box, but he had a feeling they'd go through all of them and more before their time together was over. His chest pinched. He'd miss her when he left.

A taxi dropped them off in Imerovigli, and they made their way back to the B&B. Sam's cellphone rang. He glanced at the call ID, smiled and answered, "Hey, Mack."

"Deirdre and I are on the ferry, crossing over to Santorini. We should be there this afternoon. Wyatt and Fiona are flying in about the same time. And I got word Ronin has a girlfriend."

"What?" Sam was surprised. Ronin hadn't mentioned a woman in his life. "When did that happen?"

"Apparently, he met her two years ago in Venice."

"So that's why he went to Venice from Dublin."

"You bet. He found her. He wanted to introduce you

to her, so he's bringing her to Santorini for our little mini-family reunion."

"That's great. I'm happy for him, and you and Wyatt."

"Now we just have to find you a woman."

"Don't go there," he said, glancing across at Kinsey and smiling. "I'm perfectly capable of handling that task on my own."

"Good, then we'll all have dates at dinner tonight."

Sam didn't confirm or deny his brother's speculation.

"How's the R&R going?" Mack asked.

"Good. I took lessons in sailing today."

"No kidding?" Mack laughed. "How many times did you end up in the water?"

"None, thank you. I had an excellent instructor." He winked at Kinsey as she walked alongside him, smiling.

"You did, did you? Was she as pretty as she was patient with a land-lubbing Texan?"

"I'll let you be the judge. You'll meet her at dinner tonight."

Mack hooted into the phone so loud, Sam had to hold the device away from his head to keep from losing his hearing.

"Now I wish Dierdre and I had flown in instead of taking this darned slow ferry." He snorted. "It's romantic, she said. It's a big bus on the water and takes forever. Anyway, I'll see you when we get there."

"Roger." Sam ended the call. "We need to make dinner reservations for eight this evening."

"Eight?" Kinsey stopped in her tracks.

"You, me and my three brothers and their women."

155

Sam hooked her arm and kept them moving. "They'll be here this afternoon. I'm sure with them around, we will have no problems tonight."

"Are you sure you want me to go with you? I mean, they are your brothers, and I'm...well, I'm your employee."

He stopped and pulled her into his arms. "You're more than an employee. In fact, I'm doing this all wrong. Let me start over." He held out his hand to shake. "Hi, I'm Sam Magnus. Would you go out with me tonight? As my date?"

She laughed and took his hand. "I'd love to."

"Good. Then I'll make the dinner reservations, and you can take all the time you need to primp and do what women do to get ready for a date."

"So generous of you," she said, sarcasm dripping from her words. Then she smiled. "I think I might be overwhelmed with Magnuses. Are they all as big as you?"

"Bigger." He winked. She'd be more bowled over by their rowdiness than their size. "I'm the short one in the bunch at six feet one inch."

Kinsey's eyes widened. "You're not short. Who are their women? What should I wear?"

"One of them is an event planner in San Antonio, and the other is her Irish cousin, a fashion model. I don't know anything about Ronin's lady, so your guess is as good as mine. And you can wear what you have on." He bent and pressed a kiss to her lips. "You look great."

"You have got to be kidding. I can't show up in a

bikini and shorts." She shook her head and bit down on her lip. "At the risk of being cliché, I don't have a thing to wear. Well, I do have a dress, but sheesh. A fashion model?"

"If it makes you feel better, let's go find you a kick-ass dress."

"No. You can't keep buying my clothes." She raised her hand when he started to say something else. "And don't tell me it's part of my pay as your companion. Tonight, I'm off the clock as your date. I'll wear the dress you found me in. It's the nicest one I have."

"Didn't it get ripped?"

"I'll borrow a needle and thread from Mrs. D. But you're not buying any more clothes for me."

He held up his hands. "Okay, okay. You'll make do." Sam laughed. "They're just my brothers."

That admission didn't help erase the frown from her brow, and Sam missed her smile. But he had to admit, he liked that she wanted to make a good impression on his brothers. Not that she could make a bad one. Kinsey had a way of making everyone feel good just with her smile.

As soon as they got back to the B&B, Kinsey disappeared with Mrs. D, not to be seen until an hour later.

During that time, Sam paced the room, the hallway, and even climbed to the roof to stare out over the amazing view. He didn't stay on the roof more than ten minutes. He was afraid to leave Kinsey in case someone tried to make another attempt to capture her. Besides the view wasn't nearly as impressive without Kinsey's wealth of enthusiasm for… well, just about everything.

In the short amount of time he'd known her, she'd made a huge impression. So much so, that he counted the minutes until he saw her again. He looked at his watch and climbed down the ladder to the main level of the structure and paced the hallway, wondering what could be taking her so long to patch up a little tear in a dress. He found himself jealous of the time she was spending with the landlady. Sam retreated to the room, showered and changed into his dark slacks and white polo shirt.

When Kinsey finally returned to the suite, she wore a secretive smile and carried a dark garment bag.

"I thought you weren't buying a new dress," he said.

"I didn't," she said and disappeared into the bathroom to shower.

Remembering she'd given him cart blanche for making love to her anytime he liked, still he hesitated. The sound of running water conjured memories of their morning shower and making love beneath the spray.

At that moment, he realized he hadn't thought of Leigha since the day he'd met Kinsey. Was it possible he was finally letting go?

Not just possible...he knew it was true. He'd carried his grief with him for far too long, not allowing himself to feel anything for another woman. He'd been afraid to again open his heart.

Until Kinsey and her own flavor of sunshine happened to his life. Despite the dire circumstances of their first meeting, she continued to be optimistic, fun and happy. Sure, she had her sad and frightened moments, but she didn't let them keep her down for long. The woman pulled herself back up and got on with living.

Sam had needed her to show him that life didn't have to be all gloom and doom. Yes, he had a serious job, but he didn't have to let the grimness infect his entire being.

The more he thought about how Kinsey had changed his outlook in just a couple short days, the more he wanted to be with her. Naked in the shower. He crossed the room and reached for the door when the shower shut off.

Damn.

He'd waited too long. Now, he'd have to wait until after dinner. Unless...

He knocked on the door.

Kinsey laughed on the other side. "Took you long enough."

Sam smiled, threw open the door and stood transfixed by the woman poised before him, a towel pressed to her breasts, droplets of water sliding over her skin.

"I stayed in the shower as long as I could." She sighed. "But you didn't join me."

"I'm an idiot."

"No, just a little slow on the uptake." She held out the towel. "Make yourself useful and dry me off."

He didn't have to be told twice. Sam snatched the towel from her hand.

Kinsey turned her back to him and waited.

Starting at the top of her head, he squeezed the water from her hair and smoothed the towel over her shoulders and down her back. Reaching around her with the towel, he cupped her breasts and patted away the moisture.

As he worked his way south, his cock swelled. At the rate he was heating up, he wouldn't last long. He stopped on his downward journey, his breath held in his chest and pressed his cock to her backside, praying he could contain his passion long enough to see to her needs first.

Kinsey leaned back, circling her arm around his neck. "Foreplay can be overrated," she whispered. "I want you. Inside me. Now."

In a flash, he stripped out of his clothes. Then he whipped her around and caught her face between his hands and kissed her long and hard, his shaft nudging her damp curls. "I crave you," he said against her mouth. "The whole time you were with Mrs. D, I thought about you, about us, and about doing this." He reached down, clamped his hands on the backs of her thighs and lifted her onto the edge of the sink.

She held on around his neck and wrapped her legs around his waist.

His cock pressed against her entrance, and he almost forgot to stop and think.

But Kinsey did. She reached behind her and grabbed a box, shoving it between them. "Before we get started, shouldn't you...?"

He gritted his teeth, so past ready to sheath his cock in her juices. "You're an angel." He kissed her, ripped open the box and scattered packets across the counter and into the basin. Grabbing one small packet, he tore it open and fitted the condom over his shaft. Then he was back at her entrance, sliding into her sweet, wet channel.

Her muscles tightened around him. She dug her heels into his buttocks, sending him deeper. Kinsey's head dropped back, her damp hair falling over her shoulders, the overhead light highlighting her pale, golden tan. She was so beautiful, he couldn't believe she'd chosen to give herself to him with enthusiasm and abandon.

Sam nuzzled her neck and pressed a kiss to the pulse beating so fast at the base. Her breathing was shallow, as if she couldn't quite catch her breath, and her fingers dug into his shoulders.

"Please, Sam, don't stop what you're doing. It feels so good. So right."

He pumped in and out, balancing her on the edge of the sink as he drove deeper. Almost to that special place, he stopped, blood pounding in his ears.

Kinsey blinked and stared into his eyes. "Why did you stop?"

"I want to make love to you."

"Isn't that what we were doing?"

"Sweetheart, that wasn't all we were doing. And I want this to be special."

"It *is* special." She cupped the back of his neck and pulled him down for a kiss. "Please, don't stop."

But he disengaged, lifted her off the counter and carried her into the bedroom to lay her out on the bed.

Kinsey held open her arms and parted her legs.

Sam slipped between, picking up where he left off.

On the comfort of the mattress, he thrust harder, faster and deeper, taking her to the climax with him.

As he fell back to reality, he realized he didn't want the two weeks to end. He wanted to spend more than that short amount of time with Kinsey. How could they possibly manage any kind of arrangement? She was headed back to Virginia. He was going back to Afghanistan and then redeploying to his home station of Joint Base Lewis-McChord, Washington. He'd be on the other side of the country from the woman who, in a matter of days, had turned around his life and showed him what it was really like to live.

AFTER RINSING OFF WITH SAM, Kinsey dried her hair and slipped into the dress she'd borrowed from Mrs. D, all while moving in the afterglow of making love with a man who'd captured her heart.

She refused to think past the now of their relationship, or she'd fall into a blue funk of depression. And depression wasn't her thing. The attitude accomplished little and left her feeling hopeless. She wasn't hopeless. In fact, she'd failed several times and gotten right back up and moved on, proving to herself she could accomplish anything, even when the task seemed impossible.

Once she had her long hair dried in straight lengths, she twisted it up into an elegant knot at the back of her head. Never one to wear heavy makeup, she applied a light blush to her cheeks, eye shadow and liner to her eyelids. A dash of mascara and lipstick and she was ready.

She giggled, her heart pattering in her chest, a giddy

feeling washing over her as she pulled the vintage, silver filigree, figure-hugging dress up over her hips and settled the straps on shoulders. She'd seen Michelle Pfeiffer wear a dress just like this one in one of her movies and had always dreamed of being as elegant as the beautiful movie star. Then she looked at herself in the full-length mirror and smiled. She wasn't a fashion model, but she came pretty damn close in the dress.

A soft tap on the bathroom door reminded her of the time.

Sam called out, "A taxi's waiting on the street above the B&B. Are you ready?"

She opened the door and stepped out in the matching silver strappy sandals Mrs. D loaned her along with the dress. They were a little tight, but not so much she'd be in pain the entire night. She could even dance in the low heels, if they decided to go anywhere after their dinner. The thought of waltzing again with Sam made her heart light and happy. She could almost forget that she had someone chasing her from the shadows.

Sam stood back, his brows rising up his forehead. Then he let out a long, low whistle. "Wow. Just wow."

"It belonged to Mrs. D's mother. She was much taller than Mrs. D. And she kept the matching shoes all these years." She spun in front of him to give him the full effect. "You don't think it's too old-fashioned?"

"I don't think that style will ever be considered old-fashioned." He took her hands and held her at arm's length. "You're beautiful."

She laughed. She couldn't imagine ever getting tired

of hearing his compliments "You said that when I was wearing my shorts."

"And the statement was true then just as much as it is now. You're beautiful no matter what you wear..." his voice lowered, "or don't wear." He winked. "Because you're beautiful where it counts most..." He touched a hand to his chest.

Her eyes misted at his words. "Thank you." Travis had never spoken like that. He'd never said anything as sweet and heartfelt. Being admired for her looks felt good, but to be recognized for what was inside meant more. She stretched up on her toes and kissed him. "I'm ready when you are."

He led her out of the house, careful to look in all directions and to check the shadows before proceeding. The sun was slipping into the ocean when they climbed into the taxi to the restaurant. Mrs. D arranged the reservation, assuring him her cousin, who owned the place, made the best Greek food and would treat them like family, only better.

Sam texted his brothers the location of the restaurant. They didn't need to be collected from their ports of entry, as they'd rented cars for their stays on the island. Sam suspected they wanted to spend their time touring alone with their ladies. Having spent time with Kinsey, he completely understood.

But, he was glad they all went out of their way to get together as family for a meal.

As the taxi pulled up to the curb, Sam couldn't help the grin spreading across his face. All three of his brothers stood outside the restaurant, waiting for him, the last one to arrive.

For once, he was glad he was a couple minutes late. He couldn't wait for his brothers to meet Kinsey, and she'd make a great entrance in the borrowed dress. Sam paid the driver, got out of the taxi and reached in to help Kinsey to her feet.

When he turned back to his brothers, all three were staring, their mouths open.

Mack was first to speak. "Well, Sam. We see you finally learned how to follow orders. Your commander will be so proud. Who is your gorgeous date?" With one hand behind his date's back, he extended the other. "Hi, I'm Mack, the best-looking brother of the four."

Kinsey laughed and shook his hand.

"Guys, this is Kinsey Phillips, my...f—" He was about to say fiancée but caught himself before he started a firestorm of questions and ended up saying, "friend."

"Uh-huh." Mack winked and brought his woman forward. "This is Dierdre."

"Dierdre Darcy?" Kinsey's eyes widened, and she glanced over at Sam. "When Sam said his brother was dating a model, I never expected it to be Dierdre Darcy." She shook Dierdre's hand. "Wow, you're as beautiful in person as you are on television. I'm sorry if I sound like a gushing fan. But...well...I am."

Dierdre smiled. "Thank you. And I think I have more than a little competition with you and your dress tonight. Where did you find that gem?"

Sam introduced Kinsey to his brother, Wyatt, and his new wife, Fiona, and then turned to Ronin and his lady friend. "I'd love to introduce your date, but I haven't had the pleasure myself."

Ronin slipped an arm around the dark-haired beauty's waist. "Sam, meet Isabella Pisano, my fiancée."

"You're serious?" Sam hugged his brother, clapping a hand hard on his back. "How did this happen, and we didn't know a thing about it?" He let go of his brother and hugged his future sister-in-law. "I don't know what you see in this jerk, but welcome to the family."

She laughed and smiled up at Ronin. "He's special. The man saved my life, and my father's. I guess I'll have to keep him around."

"The Pisanos need keepers." Ronin winked at Isabella. "They attract trouble."

"I imagine, with your father's wealth, you do," Dierdre commented. "I get crazy stalkers on occasion because of my work. Your family must be plagued by them."

Isabella nodded. "Sometimes, I wish I could move to America and fade into obscurity."

"Sweetheart, you're too beautiful to fade into obscurity." Ronin kissed his soon-to-be bride. "The maître d' said our table was ready when we were. Would you like to step inside?" He curved a protective arm around his fiancée and escorted her inside.

Sam smiled and nudged his brother Mack in the side. "Isabella seems to make him happy. I'm glad for him."

Mack nodded toward Kinsey, who was talking to Fiona about San Antonio. "You, too, old man. You, too."

Sam opened his mouth to set the record straight

about him and Kinsey, but Mack grabbed Dierdre's hand and led her into the restaurant.

Why should he bother to tell his brothers Kinsey was a paid companion? When they parted ways, his brothers would assume their relationship didn't work out. He preferred they thought that as the reason, than if they knew the truth.

Sam grasped Kinsey's hand in his and followed Wyatt and Fiona into the restaurant. When they reached the table to be seated, he didn't want to let go. The fact was, he didn't ever want to let go. And that was what made his stomach clench and his pulse pound against his temples.

Kinsey had managed to slip past the defenses he'd erected around his heart. Her smile and optimism washed over the mortar of the wall, eroding it away with every moment he spent with her. He didn't want their parting to be forever.

Their lives were continents apart. What other choice did he have?

KINSEY ENJOYED VISITING with Sam's brothers and their ladies. Being with them was how she'd imagined having siblings should be and what she'd always dreamed of finding—a partner in life who had the extended family she'd always wanted.

They laughed, poked fun at each other and shared information about the parents they obviously loved dearly. The women were as lively as the men and fun to be with.

A sad little knot formed in Kinsey's belly. One she would have a hard time loosening when she and Sam parted ways. She'd never again see these men, who were such a big part of Sam's life. Nor would she have the opportunity to get to know their women better.

Kinsey could imagine how they would continue to get together as an extended family whenever they could. Eventually, they'd bring their children together to play with their cousins.

And Kinsey wouldn't be a part of the happy family as it grew even bigger. She tried not to let the realization bother her. These people were his family. He was her boss, not her real fiancé. This gathering was a job, even if he'd called it a date.

Still, she laughed and smiled. How could she not? They were funny and charming, like the man she was quickly falling in love with.

As soon as the thought emerged, she sucked in a sharp breath and fought the stinging in her eyes. She looked at her hands in her lap to keep the others from seeing the shock on her face.

She *was* falling in love with Sam. How stupid could she be? He'd specifically said he was not into long-term relationships. She was to keep other women from chasing him, women wanting him to commit to more than he was willing to. His life was in the military, flying helicopters, not coming home to one woman for the rest of his days.

Not that she'd had to deflect any female attention. Kinsey suspected his justification to keeping her around might have been a ruse.

Still, she'd failed at the one job he'd asked her to do —be a companion with no strings. She wanted those strings so badly she ached with the need.

Sam leaned close and laid his hand over hers. "Are you feeling all right?"

She pasted a smile on her face and looked up, hoping he would mistake the shine in her eyes for the glare off the chandelier hanging over them and not for the tears pooling, ready to fall. "I'm fine. Your family is wonderful. You are fortunate to have each other."

His lips twisted in a wry grin. "Yeah. They're all right. I can't imagine what life would have been like if we hadn't all grown up together."

"Like I told you. It's a bit lonely." She kept that smile planted firmly on her lips, refusing to let him think she was feeling sorry for herself.

Mack tossed his napkin on his plate. "The meal was excellent, but I'd like to find my hotel and call it a night." He glanced around the table. "I think I can actually fit everyone into my rental vehicle if you need a ride back."

"What did you rent?"

"I asked for an SUV, but they only had a full-sized van left on the lot. I can seat nine people." He laughed and shrugged. "I know, it's sexy, right?"

They laughed.

"If you don't mind, that would save us waiting for a taxi to show up," Sam said.

"We took a taxi rather than searching for the place. Our vehicle is parked at the hotel," Wyatt said. "So, yes, we'd love a ride."

Ronin raised his hand. "Count us in. We rode with Wyatt and Fiona."

The men paid their bill and left the restaurant, still talking and laughing among themselves.

Kinsey liked the easy camaraderie, and loved seeing Sam happy. When she returned to the States, she would miss his smile.

The thought made her depressed and ready to call it a night. She wanted to spend her last few days with the man all to herself.

SAM HAD WATCHED Kinsey go from cheerful and openly laughing and talking with his family, to reserved and sad.

He slipped an arm around Kinsey's waist and pulled her close while they waited for Mack to bring the van to the curb.

Kinsey and Sam were first in, claiming the backseat. The others filled the seats ahead of them.

Mack drove away from the restaurant and through the crooked roads, following the GPS device directions to the address of Sam and Kinsey's B&B.

They were several streets from their destination when a full-sized black SUV passed them on the narrow street and slammed into the side of the van.

Sam wrapped his arm around Kinsey to keep her from being flung against the windows.

"What the hell?" Mack swerved, ran up on a sidewalk and almost hit the side of a building.

The vehicle that side-swiped them slowed, backed up and raced toward them.

"Hold on!" Mack shouted, shifted into reverse and backed away as fast as he could, but the other vehicle was gaining on them.

Mack turned onto a side street.

Sam pivoted, looking behind them. "This is a dead end."

"Damn." Mack shifted into Drive and would have eased forward, but a bright red Mercedes convertible passed their side street and crashed into the vehicle that had initiated the attack.

The black SUV lurched forward, but its bumper had twisted into the bumper of the Mercedes. When the SUV drove away, it took the Mercedes with it, dragging it down the street and around the next corner.

"Follow them!" Sam shouted from the rear.

Mack raced after the wrecked vehicles. When the van rounded the blind corner, they almost rammed into the back of the red convertible stalled in the middle of the street.

The driver, an older man with a shock of white hair, leaned across the console, talking with a woman with equally white hair.

All eight of the passengers in the van climbed out.

The black SUV was nowhere in sight.

"Everyone okay?" Sam asked.

"I'm okay," Kinsey said.

Deirdre rubbed her elbow. "Bruised, but alive."

Wyatt touched Fiona's temple. "We banged heads." He stared into her eyes. "Are you all right?"

She pressed a hand to her head. "Yes." Her gaze shifted to the convertible. "I'm more worried about them."

Mack and Sam assisted the elderly couple out of the convertible and called for an ambulance and a wrecker. The police came, and Detective Demopolis arrived with them.

An hour later, they were finally able to continue their journey, more subdued than the evening started.

Mack parked on the street above the B&B, and all the passengers disembarked again.

"I can't get over that driver. What possessed him to deliberately target our van?" Mack asked.

Sam glanced at Kinsey and then back toward his brothers. "I think I know why he did it."

Wyatt's lips thinned and his jaw hardened. "Explain."

"I'd like to get Kinsey out of the street. If you want to come to the B&B where I'm staying I'll tell you everything."

Kinsey's fists clenched. Once again, someone had come after her, impacting others.

Sam took her hand and led her down the steps to the B&B.

Mrs. D came out of her room as soon as she heard the crowd entering her home. "Let me get you all something to drink." She hurried to the kitchen to fetch tea and biscuits and ouzo for those who wanted something a little stronger.

When all of Sam's brothers and their ladies were seated at a table in the dining room, Kinsey excused herself, claiming she wanted to get out of the shoes that

173

were killing her feet. She left the group, feeling like the black cloud had spread around Mack's family and was increasing in size with each passing day.

Back in their room, she stripped out of the shoes and borrowed dress and pulled on a pair of jeans, sneakers and the Santorini T-shirt Sam purchased their first day together.

She stared at the suitcase she'd brought with her to Greece, containing everything she owned. If she were smart, she'd pack up and leave before anyone else got hurt.

As the idea took hold, she knew what she had to do. While Sam filled in his brothers on what had happened over the past few days, she could pack her things and sneak out the door. She wouldn't have to walk past the dining room and they wouldn't know she'd gone until she was too far away for them to catch up to her.

And then what? She didn't have any money, and she hadn't earned her flight back to the US.

What about the bad guys?

She'd have to be vigilant and careful not to give anyone an opportunity to nab her. She'd have to rely on her self-defense skills and avoid being drugged.

Her lips tightened. It didn't really matter what happened to her, as long as Sam and his family remained safe. With her out of the picture, the people targeting her would have no reason to bother Sam.

She jerked her suitcase out of the closet, threw it onto the bed and jammed her clothing inside, leaving out the things Sam purchased. Other than the Santorini

T-shirt, she wouldn't take those items. She hadn't earned them

Kinsey hung up the dress she'd borrowed from Mrs. D in the garment bag and sat at the little table to write two quick notes. One thanking Mrs. D for her hospitality and the loan of her beautiful dress. The other to Sam.

A tear slipped down her cheek onto the paper as she folded it. She placed it on his pillow, grabbed her suitcase and left the room she'd shared with Sam, her chest so tight she could barely breathe.

She was doing the right thing. Leaving was the only way to keep Mrs. D, Sam and his family safe. She should have done it much sooner. Sam wouldn't have almost been run over by a car or bruised his ribs and knuckles fighting off the bad guys. Mrs. D's home wouldn't have been broken into, and Mack's rental van wouldn't have been side-swiped, almost killing everyone Sam loved so much.

Kinsey slipped into the hallway and paused, listening to Sam's warm, rich tones as he shared the details of her disastrous hours in Greece. He owed it to his brothers to let them know why they'd been targeted. But Kinsey still hurt to know she was responsible for all their problems.

If she had been more aware of her surroundings in Athens and held onto her purse...If she hadn't agreed to work for the Martins and allowed them to bring her to Santorini, none of this would have happened. And she wouldn't have been kidnapped, nor would she have met Sam.

Even if she tried, she couldn't begin to regret meeting Sam. He'd shown her that she wasn't done living. That she still had a lot of love in her heart to give and that honorable men existed in the world. She just had to find one who believed in falling in love and living happily ever after.

But she'd never find another man just like Sam. When he'd loosened up, he'd demonstrated a happier, more adventurous man, and his smile had been well worth waiting for. She'd miss him.

A chair scraped across the tile floor, reminding Kinsey she had to leave before she was discovered. Sam would try to stop her, claiming she wasn't the one at fault.

But by staying, she knew she brought bad luck and bad men to this wonderful family. As quietly as she could, she tiptoed down the hallway toward the back and exited the building, closing the door behind her.

With a plan in mind and the determination to see it through, she set off.

She just had to find a place to hide near the port until morning when she would search for someone who could take her back to the mainland. From there, she'd contact the U.S. Embassy and beg them to help her get home. If she had to take out a loan to purchase a ticket, she'd pay it all back as soon as she got a job.

Kinsey zigzagged through the narrow passages leading across the side of the hill to the road that would ultimately lead to the port. She had gone past several buildings, moving quickly when the hairs on the back of her neck prickled. A shadow shifted and moved before the shape of a person emerged.

No way. She wouldn't be the victim again. Not when Sam had done so much to keep her safe. She turned to face her attacker, holding her suitcase in front of her like a shield.

"Kinsey?" a feminine voice said from the darkness. "Oh, thank God you're okay." Lois Martin stepped into the starlight, her hands pressed to her chest, her eyes red-rimmed from crying. "They took my children. Help me, please."

13

———

SAM BROUGHT his brothers up-to-date on what had happened since he'd arrived on Santorini and how he'd met Kinsey. He didn't tell them he'd hired her to be his companion or that she was earning her ticket back to Virginia. "I think the driver of the SUV might have been after the van because Kinsey was in it."

"Damn," Wyatt said. "Why didn't you let us know sooner?"

Sam gave his brother a wry grin. "You were supposed to be on your honeymoon. Besides, we turned over the matter to the police. They know a human trafficking ring is based off this island. They just haven't been able to capture those responsible." He glanced around, searching for Kinsey, his pulse quickening. She should have been back from changing out of her dress by then. "I'll be right back."

Sam rose from his chair and strode toward the room he'd shared with Kinsey. The haven where he'd made love to her a few short hours ago. Had he embarrassed her by telling his brothers about her tangle with the kidnappers?

"Kinsey," he called out as he pushed open the door and entered the room. The bed was neatly made, the dark garment bag hung on the closet door and everything was tidy. Too tidy, including the bed where they'd made love before they'd gone out for dinner.

Mrs. D made beds earlier in the day. Had she been in the room while they went out to eat?

That's when he noticed her suitcase was missing from the closet and there was a folded paper propped on his pillow. A sense of dread washed over him as he crossed the room and lifted it in his hands. He unfolded the note, and his heart sank deeper with every word he read.

Dear Sam,

I've loved every minute of our time together. You are the kind of man every woman dreams of, and I was lucky enough to have you for a few short days. But I can't complete my obligation if, by doing so, I put you and your beautiful family in danger. Don't come after me. Doing so will only prolong the inevitable. I hope you find the peace you so deserve and someone who will love and appreciate what a wonderful, adventurous man you are. And don't marry her unless she makes you smile.

Kinsey

"MACK! WYATT! RONIN!" Sam grabbed his knife and ran out of the room.

All three of his brothers met him in the hallway.

"What's wrong?" Mack asked.

Wyatt touched his brother's arm. "Where's Kinsey?"

"She's gone." He handed the note to Ronin, and shoved his Ka-Bar knife into the scabbard strapped to his calf. "We have to find her."

"We're with you," Wyatt said.

Mack nodded. "Damn right. She's one of us."

"You really care for her, don't you?" Ronin asked.

Sam's heart swelled in his chest. He hadn't realized until now, but yes, he did care for Kinsey. A great deal. "I know it's crazy. I've only known her a short time, but she's perfect."

"And she makes you smile," Wyatt said. "I didn't think anyone could do that after Leigha died."

"Me, either, but Kinsey can. She could make a statue smile just by standing beside it. The woman is amazing, and we have to find her." He pushed past his brothers and ran out of the building.

He glanced left, then right. Where would she have gone at night? She didn't have any money, nor did she have the ticket to fly home. She'd left the printed confirmation on the table in their room. Even if she wanted to, she couldn't change the reservation without paying a fee. Without a credit card, she couldn't do that, either. Her only option was to find someone to ferry her back to the mainland, which meant she'd head for the dock to see if she could catch a free ride with one of the boats going that way.

"Which way would she have gone?" Ronin asked.

"To the port. If she wants off the island, she'd have to

go by water." He pulled his phone from his pocket and dialed the number the detective provided.

"Athan, I need your help. Kinsey is missing. She might be heading for the port. I'm afraid whoever is after her might find her before she gets there."

"I'm on my way," Athan said.

"I'll meet you on the main road. We're heading down now."

He and his brothers split up and took different paths through the twisting corridors up to the main road running along the ridge of the island.

"See anything?" Sam asked as he stood on the side of the road, breathing hard, his heart heavy.

Mack, Ronin, Isabella and Wyatt all shook their heads.

"Nothing," Mack confirmed.

The more time that passed, the more anxious Sam became. Kinsey could be anywhere. What if someone dragged her into one of the buildings he'd passed? He and his brothers couldn't begin to search all of them.

If she made it to the main road, she could have been picked up by the men in the SUV who'd rammed the van earlier. In which case, she'd be a lot farther away.

A vehicle pulled up to where the four men stood on the side of the road, and Detective Athan Demopolis stepped out. "You didn't find her?"

Sam shook his head.

"I got a lead over an hour ago. All my units were too busy handling other incidents to check it out. It might be nothing, but at this point…"

"Anything is better than nothing," Sam finished.

"What do you have?" Wyatt asked.

"There is a small warehousing building near the Port of Athinios. Cargo is staged going in and out at that point. We received an anonymous call today reporting someone trespassing in that area. The yard has a fence around it, and the gate is usually locked, but the lock had been removed and the gate was unsecured. We sent a unit, but they were called away before they could complete a thorough investigation."

"If they are trafficking people in and out of Santorini, it makes sense they would take them through the port where boats and ships can dock," Wyatt said.

Sam clenched his fists. The clue was a long shot, but it was the only one they had. "Let's check it out."

KINSEY KNEW AS SOON as she agreed to follow Lois Martin that she was making a big mistake. But the look on the woman's face and the tearstains on her cheeks found their way past Kinsey's defenses. She didn't care for the woman, but the kids couldn't choose their parents. "What happened?" Kinsey asked as she followed Lois through the narrow alleys up to the main road.

"We were at the hotel a couple days ago and men took my children. They said if we wanted them back, we had to check out of the Porto Takisi and do everything they said."

Kinsey's heart hurt for the kids. They had to be terrified. "Where's Mr. Martin?"

"They're holding him, as well. They let me go to bring you back."

Kinsey stopped in her tracks. "Are you telling me that I'm the trade? Me for your family?"

She nodded. "I couldn't see any other way around it. They threatened to kill my husband and children if I went to the police." Lois grabbed her arm. "Please, you have to come with me. Their lives depend on it."

"What about *my* life?" Kinsey demanded.

Tears flowed from Lois's eyes. "They're children…"

Kinsey half-turned to walk back to the B&B where Sam and his brothers were. But she'd left to keep them safe. Going back would only embroil them further in her situation. How could she make everything right? She was only one person. A woman worth more to the captors than an entire family they were willing to destroy to get her.

If she lived through that evening and managed to escape, she planned to get fat and dye her hair mud brown. Being blond was not more fun when your life was being threatened by human traffickers.

"I'm going to the police," Kinsey said.

Lois clutched her arm. "You can't. They'll kill my babies."

"Even if you offer me in trade, we don't know that they won't renege and take me *and* the kids anyway."

Lois's fingers dug into her arm. "The kidnappers said that if we notified the police, they'd kill them. Please, they're just children."

Kinsey didn't trust Lois, but the woman was very convincing. She'd find a way to help Lois, if not for the woman herself and her husband, then for the children. They hadn't lived long enough to deserve to be exterminated by ruthless bastards. Or worse, sold into the sex slave trade.

Her heart squeezed hard in her chest at that thought. An image of Lilly and Dalton playing on the beach swam into Kinsey's memory. They'd played in the surf and sand with joyous abandon.

Kinsey couldn't turn her back on them. If it meant trading her life for theirs, so be it. But she'd do her damnedest to escape. She had no desire to be sold into the sex trade, either. And she wouldn't walk blindly into a trap that would sacrifice her freedom and buy nothing for those poor kids.

Her heart heavy and her nerves stretched, Kinsey followed Lois to the main road where a black SUV with a crushed bumper pulled out of a side road and stopped beside them.

Two big men, probably the ones who'd originally kidnapped Kinsey, jumped out.

Kinsey backed up a few steps, ready to run. "What guarantee do I have that you'll free the Martin family?"

"None." Lois's face hardened, and she jerked her head toward the SUV. "Get her."

Kinsey's pulse rocketed and adrenaline raced through her veins. She took off running, glad she'd changed into her sneakers. But she wasn't fast enough. The men caught her all too soon, tackling her like football players.

She hit the ground so hard, the air was knocked from her lungs. As she skidded across the stone walkway, she skinned her knees through her jeans. Pain was the least of her worries. She had to get away from these people.

How could she be so stupid as to trust Lois Martin? The bitch'd been in on the whole heist from the beginning when she'd sat beside her on the bench in Athens.

As the men loaded her into the SUV, she could only be thankful for one thing—this time, Sam wouldn't have to fight his way through these men. If he read her letter, he'd know she'd left of her own free will. Even so, would he come looking for her? In the back of her mind, Kinsey held out hope.

The SUV drove south, as far as Kinsey could tell. They'd stuffed a rag in her mouth, tied her wrists behind her back, using the scarf Lois had worn, and then secured her ankles with duct tape. Then they'd tossed her into the back of the vehicle on the floor. She tried to sit up to look out the window, but every time they rounded a corner, she was thrown across the floor again, bumping her head against the sides of the vehicle.

She could tell the van was winding downhill, traversing back and forth. From her knowledge of the island, she'd bet they were heading down to the little Port of Athinios where the ferries landed and cargo for the island could be loaded and unloaded. If she didn't get loose soon, she'd be hauled off in the belly of a ship never to be found again.

How she wished things could have been different. What if the Martins hadn't been in on the kidnapping and cared about their children and wanted her to be an au pair? Would she have met Sam? And if she had, would they have found the same spark and physical connection?

She wanted so badly to see him again. To have him wrap his arms around her and hold her until this nightmare went away. But she was the master of her fate. Sam might not come to find her. If she wanted to escape the awful plan her captors had for her, she had to make it happen all by herself.

Kinsey worked the rag out of her mouth and, with the tips of her fingernails, tore at the tape binding her ankles. She practically had to contort to reach the tape, but she possessed a strong will and always looked for solutions to her problems. If they didn't drug her, she had a chance. If she got out of this situation, she'd go back to Sam and convince him of a future where the two of them could be together.

The vehicle stopped, and the big guys got out, opened the back of the SUV and dragged her out, grabbing her arms and legs. They'd parked behind some buildings between stacks of crushed corrugated cardboard and wooden pallets.

Kinsey didn't scream, knowing that if they were smart enough to figure out she'd dislodged the rag from her mouth, they'd shove it right back in. Instead, she studied her surroundings in the light from the stars overhead. She smelled the salty, fishy scent of the sea and heard waves gently lapping against the shore.

They carried her to a small building with few windows and what appeared to be only one door.

Lois unlocked the door and held it open for the men to take her inside.

The building contained a variety of wooden crates large enough to ship household goods and furniture. Big enough to hold a full-grown woman. Maybe two or three.

Her heart beat faster as her gaze shot around the room, searching for some way to extricate herself from this horrible dilemma.

"Put her in with the others." Lois nodded toward a door at the far end of the building. "And that's it. We met our quota. I'll call for pickup." She pulled a cellphone from her pocket and turned away.

Her henchmen carried Kinsey across the warehouse and dumped her in a room the size of a walk-in closet. The space smelled of disinfectant and cleaning fluid.

She fell on her side, pain shooting through her shoulder, but she didn't let it daunt her.

The door closed before she could see who the others were. She lay for a moment, getting her bearings, and then spoke softly. "Hello?"

A whimper sounded behind her. Another from nearer where her head lay against the concrete floor.

"Who's there?" she asked, her voice shaking. The darkness frightened her more than the people within.

"There are three of us," a woman said with a decidedly British accent. "I'm Alaina. Brigid and Helene are here, as well."

"Are you all tied up?" Kinsey asked.

"Yes," Alaina said.

"With what?"

"My hands are bound behind my back with rope. I

187

can't get it loose and the more I try, the tighter it gets. I can barely feel my fingers."

Someone spoke in another language that sounded Swedish or Dutch.

"Brigid and Helene are bound with duct tape."

"If we help each other, we should be able to free our hands." Determined not to remain a victim, Kinsey used an elbow to push herself to a sitting position. "Brigid, let me see if I can work the tape loose."

Alaina translated and a slight figure inched across the floor to sit with her back to Kinsey.

Kinsey pulled and poked at the tape with her fingernails, making minimal progress. But she couldn't give up. "Alaina, I know you can barely move your fingers, but try and work through the tape on Helene's wrists. If we can get one of us loose, that one can free the rest."

Kinsey worked silently and as fast as she could. The tape was on tight, but she finally found the end and yanked to unwind enough that Brigid could separate her wrists. "Hurry, untie us," she whispered.

They had to be free and ready to make a break for it before Lois's pickup crew came for them.

Brigid struggled with the scarf, finally working out the knot and pulling it off her wrists. Kinsey let go of the breath she'd been holding, hope surging from within. With her hands unbound, Kinsey ripped the tape from around her ankles and helped Alaina liberate Helene.

While Helene and Brigid worked the knot out of the ropes on Alaina's wrists, Kinsey felt her way around the room. She found mops, buckets, spray bottles and jugs of cleaning fluid. She gathered items and scooted them toward the door. She couldn't find another exit so they had to work with the only existing one and be ready to attack their abductors. Whispering commands, she set the other women to work pouring fluid into the spray bottles and dismantling the mops so that they could use the long poles as weapons.

When Lois and her goons opened the door again, they would be in for a surprise. Hopefully, they wouldn't be armed with guns. Even then, the women were better off dead than sold into the sex trade.

Kinsey prepared her plan of attack, coached her makeshift army and waited for their moment to launch their escape strategy. She'd be damned if she let anyone else take advantage of her or the other ladies trapped in the closet.

14

SAM SAT in the passenger seat of the van as Mack careened around the hairpin curves leading down the side of the hill to the Port of Athinios. He craned his neck with each turn, hoping to catch a glimpse of the buildings below, but they weren't quite close enough to see to the bottom. Dread built with each passing second. Regret formed a hard knot in the pit of his belly. He should have kept Kinsey in sight at all times.

When the van finally made it to the coastal road, they slowed, following Detective Demopolis. He'd called for backup, but Sam and his brothers refused to wait.

Isabella, who'd spent time in Syria fighting for abused women there, insisted on accompanying them. Fiona and Dierdre wanted to come, but they stayed behind to keep Mrs. D calm.

With their own small army, the Magnuses could take out whoever got in the way, even though the only weapons they carried were their Ka-Bar knives. Isabella had pepper spray and a Taser.

Sam prayed their adversaries weren't more heavily armed.

The detective motioned for them to park far enough away from the designated location that their vehicles would be hidden by buildings. The team would go in on foot. If the kidnappers were there, they'd be surprised. If not, they'd have to start all over in their search.

In Sam's mind, the clock was ticking. His pulse raced and his muscles tensed. They had to find Kinsey before she left the island. Once off Santorini, she'd be impossible to locate.

The men and Isabella climbed out of the van and hurried to join the detective. He told them the layout to expect, and they split up into two teams. One would go through the front gate. The other team would come around from behind and slip through the back gate.

When he flew, Sam relied heavily on communications equipment. Without it, he felt as if he was flying blind. But he wouldn't let the handicap stop him. Kinsey could be in there. He'd move Heaven and Earth to get to her.

And when he did, he'd tell her how he felt and that he thought they would be good together, even if their relationship was long distance for much of the time. He liked her. A lot. Maybe even loved her. He sure as hell wanted to give love another chance. As long as the romance was with Kinsey. Her smiles rivaled the sunshine and made him happier than he'd been in a very long time.

He wouldn't let this be the end.

Sam accompanied the detective and Mack through the front entrance. Someone had hooked a combination lock on the links of a heavy chain, but it wasn't clicked shut.

Sam eased the lock free and lowered the chain quietly so that it didn't bang against the chain-link fence. Then he slipped through the gate and into the shadow of a nearby building.

The three of them moved from one structure to the next by chasing the shadows, with Sam in the lead.

As they neared the back of the complex, Sam saw a dark vehicle parked between a stack of crushed cardboard and a stack of wooden pallets.

The back end of the vehicle had been smashed, and the bumper was missing.

Bingo. They'd found the SUV that had tried to run their van off the road.

His heart pounded against his ribs. Kinsey had to be in one of the buildings. Sam prayed the kidnappers hadn't had time to get her onto a boat and off the island.

He tried the door on the first building they came to. The knob was securely locked. Sam pressed his ear to the wall but couldn't hear any noises coming from within.

Mack stood on his toes at the side of the structure to peer into a small, dirty window. He dropped down, shaking his head.

Empty.

Sam gave a silent signal to Wyatt, Ronin and Isabella. They eased through the back gate and searched the building on the other side of the yard, moving through one at a time.

As Sam worked his way toward the black SUV, the hairs on the back of his neck stood at attention. His instinct told him he was getting closer. It also told him that a hostage rescue wasn't going to be easy.

Lights glared from the road and a delivery truck slid stopped at the entrance to the warehouse yard. A man dropped to the ground, opened the gate and held it wide while the truck drove through.

Sam, along with the rest of their rescue team, shrank into the shadows. When the truck stopped in front of the small building nearest the SUV, the driver and another man dropped down from the cab. They walked to the rear and flung open the back.

The door of the building opened, and a woman stepped out along with the two men Sam recognized as the ones who'd been kidnapping Kinsey the first time.

Sam started forward, his fists clenched.

Detective Demopolis grabbed his arm and held him back, motioning to one of the men. "He's armed," the detective whispered. "And so is she."

Sam looked closer. The woman held a handgun at her side as if to warn the newcomers she couldn't be easily intimidated. He saw movement from the other side of the group in the open. Ronin was easing nearer.

"I have to get going." Sam pushed past the detective's hold. Moving in the shadows, he crept along the side of the adjacent building and waited for the moment the group in the yard wasn't looking and made the move to cross the open space between the side of the smaller building. He circled around to the back and didn't find another door. If he wanted to get inside, he'd have to go through the people standing there.

By the time he'd worked his way forward to the end of the building closest to the party out front, Athan and Mack joined him.

He peered around the corner, careful not to make any sudden moves that would alert the kidnappers to their presence. He looked for Ronin, Wyatt and Isabella. At first, he couldn't see any of them. Then Ronin poked out his head from the opposite corner of the building.

They were all in place. Now was the time to make their move. Rushing them from both directions hopefully would confuse the people with weapons and give the team sufficient time to disarm them.

"I have the man with the rifle," Mack said.

"I'll take the woman," Sam responded. "Ready?" He didn't wait for Mack or the detective to respond. With a deep breath, he took off running.

Mack, the faster brother, sprinted past him and hit the man with the rifle in the side, like a football linebacker going in for the tackle.

The woman Sam targeted darted for the door to the building and ducked inside before Sam reached her.

The other man from the truck dove in behind her.

The door slammed in Sam's face and a lock clicked in place. Sam didn't even look back at the sounds of a fight that ensued. He reared back and kicked the door as hard as he could. It didn't budge. The woman must have thrown a deadbolt on the other side. He kicked again, only managing to jolt the hell out of his leg.

Kinsey had to be inside. Why else would the woman have barricaded herself in the building?

Sam realized he'd have to use a lot more force than his foot could provide. He turned in time to see the detective kick the rifle out of reach of the man Mack had tackled.

Ronin had his hands full with one of the big guys who'd attacked Kinsey, while Wyatt pinned the other.

Isabella grabbed the rifle from the ground and ran for the door. "Get back!" she yelled. Then she aimed the muzzle downward at the space between the door handle and the doorframe and pulled the trigger. The doorjamb splintered.

Sam kicked at the door, but it still wouldn't open.

Isabella aimed and fired another round. This time, the doorjamb disintegrated, and the door swung inward.

Sam and Isabella jumped to the side of the door.

Several shots were fired from within, hitting the back of the truck.

Sam waited a moment before diving through the opening and rolled to the side.

Isabella did the same, diving to the opposite side.

More shots sounded, but Sam didn't give a rat's ass if the woman was aiming at him. He had to find Kinsey.

The lights were turned off in the building, making it difficult to locate the man and woman who'd run inside. And Sam didn't know if they were the only Tangos they had to be concerned with. "Kinsey!" he yelled and held his breath, praying for a response.

"Sam?"

He heard her voice call out, as if muffled by a wall or door, and his heart started to beat all over again.

Isabella moved. A click sounded, and the building was bathed in light from a row of fluorescent bulbs hung from the ceiling.

Sam spotted the woman with the gun on the opposite end of the room. She flung open a door and pointed her gun inside. "Come any closer, and I'll shoot her," she shouted.

Sam froze, his heart in his throat. "Don't shoot!"

The woman smirked. "Then get out, and take your friends with you."

Before Sam could take one step forward or backward, a long stick exploded out of the darkness of the closet where the woman stood. It connected with the hand holding the gun.

The gun went off as it was lifted into the air and smashed to the ground.

Kinsey was the first out the door, wielding what appeared to be a broom or mop handle. She used it to whack the woman in the side of the head, and then she shoved her backward.

The woman tripped and fell on her back.

Kinsey pounced, slamming the broom handle over the woman's throat and pinning her to the ground. "Move and I'll break your neck," Kinsey threatened, her voice low and rough like a lion's growl.

Several young women jumped through the door, armed with spray bottles. They cornered the man who'd followed the woman into the building and sprayed liquid in his face.

He screamed and covered his eyes.

"Kinsey, do you need help?" Sam called out.

"Not yet," Kinsey responded from her perch straddling the woman who'd threatened to kill her. "Grab her gun."

Sam retrieved the woman's handgun and performed a quick search of the interior of the structure, looking for anyone hiding in the shadowy corners. When he was certain no one else would jump out and shoot them he crossed to where Kinsey held the woman pinned to the floor.

Detective Demopolis entered the building and hurried over to the man surrounded by the women with spray bottles. After he secured the man's wrists behind his back with zip-ties, the detective crossed to Kinsey and cuffed the woman she'd subdued.

Sam helped Kinsey to her feet and wrapped her in his arms. The sense of relief that washed over him made his knees shake and his eyes burn. "God, I thought I'd never see you again."

Shaking her head, she chuckled. "That was my intention. But I wasn't planning on going out quite like this."

He tipped up her head and stared down into her blue eyes. "Please, don't leave me again."

She wrapped her arms around his waist. "I couldn't stay. Not when I was the one they wanted. I couldn't let them hurt you and your family."

His chest swelled at her reason.

Kinsey hadn't been thinking of herself. She'd cared

enough about Sam and his family that she'd walked away to protect them.

His arms tightened around her, and he rested his cheek against her hair. "But you left. Without saying goodbye."

"I wrote a note…"

He shook his head. "Not good enough. You didn't give me a chance to talk you out of leaving."

She laughed, her voice catching on a sob. "I knew if I stayed, I couldn't walk away. And now, you're making our separation harder than ever."

"Then don't walk away." He brushed his lips across hers.

"But you said from the beginning you weren't into commitment." She raised her hands to lace behind his head. "You don't know how hard it was to leave the first time. In less than two weeks, I have to do it all over again."

His gut clenched. "No, you don't."

"You have a job to do. You don't want a long-term relationship."

"I was wrong?" He kissed her again.

"About the job or the relationship?" She asked, her eyes swimming in tears. "And please…don't make me cry. My eyes get all ugly and red." She sniffed.

"Darlin', I never want to make you cry. You brought back the sunshine into my life. I want your smile and laughter. I want you to teach me more about sailing."

She snorted. "You could hire someone to teach you how to sail."

"I already did. And I like my instructor. In fact," he

leaned forward to whisper into her ear. "I'm falling in love with her."

Her fingers tightened on the back of his neck. "You wouldn't tell me that just to make me feel better, would you?"

Hope flared inside him. She hadn't argued or rejected his comment about falling in love with her. "I'd tell you that to make *me* feel better. *You* make me feel better and more alive than I've felt in a long time. I don't want to let that go. I don't want to let *you* go." Then he kissed her long and deep, sweeping past her teeth to caress her tongue and taste her very essence. She was the one he'd been waiting for. The woman who awakened him to the possibilities of happily ever after.

"And I don't want to let you go, either." She stared up into his eyes. "Do you think two people can fall in love this fast?"

He nodded, happiness flowing through him, making him feel like he'd won the lottery. "I do."

She raised up on her toes and kissed him. "Then I think I'm falling in love with you."

"Hey, you two. Get a room," Mack said.

Reluctantly, Sam lifted his head and glanced at his brother.

"We're cleared to leave. So, if you want a ride back to Mrs. D's, we're leaving."

Sam took Kinsey's hand firmly in his and walked out of the building and into the brightest starlight he could imagine.

"What about the other women?" Kinsey asked, glancing over her shoulder.

"They were reported missing in the past forty-eight hours," Mack said. "The detective is arranging for their transport so they can be reunited with their families."

"They were amazing," Kinsey said. "We all worked together to free ourselves."

"You're amazing," Sam said as he squeezed her hand. "I should have known you would get yourself out of any situation."

"And I should have known you'd find me." She leaned into him and let him lead her to where the van was parked a couple buildings away.

The drive up the hill from the port was slower than the mad rush down. Soon, they were back at the B&B where they shared the story of what went down with Fiona and Dierdre.

Mrs. D offered rooms to the entire Magnus family, but Wyatt, Mack and Ronin had already made reservations at another resort and spa with infinity pools and massage therapists. Mrs. D laughed and admitted she couldn't compete with their amenities, but they were welcome to come have tea with her anytime.

The brothers promised to meet for dinner the next evening for one last reunion before all but Sam would leave the island.

Sam loved his brothers, but he couldn't wait for them to leave so he could be alone with Kinsey in the room they shared. Once inside, with the door closed, he folded her into his arms. "Kinsey Phillips, you're fired."

"Fired?" She stared, her brow knitting in a confused frown.

"I don't want you as a paid companion."

200

"But how am I supposed to earn my ticket back to Virginia?"

"And about that? Why does the location have to be Virginia? Have you considered starting over in the state of Washington? Specifically, around Ft. Lewis? The area's a lot prettier than Virginia, and you could still be near the water."

She smiled, lighting the entire room. "Are you asking me to commit to a long-term relationship with a certain helicopter pilot?"

He took a deep breath and gladly took that huge step. "I am."

"I don't want you to feel trapped in a relationship that won't make you happy."

Sam traced a finger along her cheek and tucked a strand of her hair behind her ear. "I will never feel trapped with you. And we can take it slowly, if you like. Get to know each other better. Fall in love over a long time...like maybe a month or two."

"Or two weeks on Santorini?"

"Or two weeks on Santorini." He lifted her into his arms and carried her to their bed where they made crazy, passionate love.

Later that night, his cellphone rang. He glanced at the caller ID and smiled.

Colonel Cooley.

"Sir?" he answered.

"Are you still following my orders?"

"Sorry, sir, I'm on vacation and deep in a session of rest and relaxation. I can't talk now. I'm busy following my commander's orders. I'll see you when I get back."

He could hear his commander's chuckle as he ended the call and turned off the ringer. "Now, where were we?"

Kinsey curled her hand behind his head and drew him close. "Right where we were supposed to be." And she kissed him.

Enjoy other military books by Elle James

Hearts & Heroes Series
Wyatt's War (#1)
Mack's Witness (#2)
Ronin's Return (#3)
Sam's Surrender (#4)
Brotherhood Protector Series
Montana SEAL (#1)
Bride Protector SEAL (#2)
Montana D-Force (#3)
Cowboy D-Force (#4)
Montana Ranger (#5)
Montana Dog Soldier (#6)
Montana SEAL Daddy (#7)
Montana Ranger's Wedding Vow (#8)
Montana Rescue

MONTANA SEAL

BROTHERHOOD PROTECTORS BOOK #1

New York Times & USA Today
Bestselling Author

ELLE JAMES

New York Times & USA Today Bestselling Author

ELLE JAMES

MONTANA
SEAL

BROTHERHOOD PROTECTORS

"MONTANA, TAKE POINT," Big Bird said. "You'll need to move in fast, once I take out the guard."

Hank Patterson, aka Montana, adjusted his night vision goggles, gripped his M4A1 rifle with the SOP Mod upgrade and rose from his concealed position on the edge of the Iraqi village. U.S. Army intelligence guys had it from a trusted source that an influential leader of the ISIS movement had set up shop in the former home of the now dead Sheik Ghazi Sattar, a paramount chief of the Rishawi tribe. The once palatial estate had taken mortar fire from the Islamic State of Iraq and Syria—or ISIS—rebels. The sheik and his fighters had succumbed to the overpowering forces and died in battle.

In the process, ISIS had gained a stronghold in the village and captured an aid worker the U.S. government wanted returned. When ISIS offered the aid worker in exchange for captured members of their party, the current administration held to its stand that it didn't negotiate with terrorists.

That's where the navy SEALs came in. Under the cover of night, armed with limited intel and specialized sound-suppressed weapons, SEAL Team 10 was to infiltrate the compound, kill the leader, Abu Sayyaf, and liberate the aid worker, who happened to be the Secretary of Defense's niece.

Piece of cake, Montana assured himself. This was what he lived for. Or at least he'd been telling himself that for the past year. He was coming up on the anniversary of his enlistment, and he had to decide whether to get out of the military or re-up. Reenlistment meant more wear and tear on his body and more chances of being shot, blown up or bored out of his mind. When they were called to duty, the missions were intense, yet the downtime gave him too much time to think.

Besides, he wasn't getting any younger. If he didn't leave active duty, he'd end up training SEALs, rather than conducting missions. That would give him even more time to think about what could have been back in his home state.

How many years had it been since he'd visited home? Eight? Ten? Hell, it had been eleven years since he'd been back to Montana. He could remember that defining night like it was yesterday. He'd just broken up with Sadie. He was hurting and wondering if they were insane to give up the best thing that had ever happened to them. Then he and his father had a big blow out. His father called him a lazy, good-for-nothing son and told him to get to work or get out.

Looking back, breaking up with Sadie had been the best thing, all the way around. She'd gone on to become a Hollywood mega-star, and Montana had gotten the hell away from his father, joined the Navy and become a member of an elite force. Life had turned out pretty good for them both.

So why did he still think about home...and Sadie? Hell, he knew why. Every time his reenlistment came up, he started thinking about home. Most of his friends from high school were married and had children. He'd always wanted kids, but SEALs made crummy parents and spouses. They were gone most of the time, sometimes without a way to contact loved ones back home.

"Be ready." Lieutenant Mike lay next to Montana. "Big Bird, hold your fire until I give the cue."

"Roger," Big Bird responded.

New to the team, Lt. Mike wasn't new to being a SEAL. With four years and ten deployments under his belt, he was a seasoned warrior, although his recent marriage seemed to have slowed him down. He wasn't as quick to leap into a bad situation. And if rumor had it right, his wife was expecting their first child.

"Let's do it," Lt. Mike said.

The muted thump of Big Bird's rifle discharging was Montana's signal to take off.

The ISIS guard who had been pacing the top of a roof slumped forward and fell to the ground with a soft whomp.

Montana held his breath, straining his ears for the

shout of alarm that didn't come. With the sentry elimi-
nated, Montana had a clear path to the wall. He took off
running, hunkered low, his weapon ready, his gaze
scanning the top of the wall, searching for the tell-tale
green heat signature of a warm body through his night
vision goggles.

Swede and Stingray were right behind him.

His skin crawled and his gut clenched. Something
didn't feel right. But the mission had to move forward.
They had an enemy target to acquire and a woman to
rescue before they could go home to Virginia.

Montana knelt at the base of the wall, slung his rifle
over his arm, cupped his hands and bent low.

Swede ran up to him, stepped into his cupped hands
and launched himself into the air. He hooked his arms
over the top, dragged himself over and dropped to the
ground below.

Stingray came next, then Nacho, Irish and
Lt. Mike.

Big Bird would remain on top of a nearby building
and be their eyes and ears for anyone approaching the
compound. He'd also provide cover fire for them as
they exited with the aid worker.

Lieutenant Mike, the newest member of the team,
paused at the top of the wall and reached a hand down
to Montana, pulling him up and over.

Swede and Nacho had already moved forward to the
main building, one side of which was caved in, like an
open wound. The remaining walls bore pockmarks
from bullets and shrapnel. The huge wooden door still
stood, closed and strangely unguarded.

"It doesn't feel right," Swede whispered into Montana's headset.

"Stay the course," Lt. Mike responded.

"Going in," Swede acknowledged and slipped into the broken corner of the structure, climbing over the half-wall still standing.

Nacho waited a moment until Swede said, "Clear."

Nacho hopped over the wall and through the crumbled bricks, disappearing into the gaping hole.

Lt. Mike went next, then Montana. Irish brought up the rear.

Once inside, what walls still stood seemed to close in on Montana.

Lt. Mike forged ahead, hurrying past the crumbled bricks and mortar.

Swede and Nacho stood at a door leading deeper into the once ornate residence. Swede wedged a knife into the doorjamb, while Nacho aimed his rifle at the door, ready for anything. A quick jab and the lock gave. Swede nodded to Nacho, yanked open the door and stood back. Nothing happened. Nacho dove through the opening and to the side, leaving room for Swede to follow. Lt. Mike entered next.

The team moved through the building, room by room.

"There's nobody here," Montana said.

"Then why the guard on top of the building?" Big Bird asked, still connected via the two-way radios in their helmets.

"Suppose it's a trap?" Irish asked.

"We have to check all rooms." Lt. Mike said.

Montana fought a groan. The place had to be over twelve thousand square feet. And that didn't include any underground bunkers that might be a part of the former Sheik's defense plan. Lt. Mike was right. If they didn't check all the rooms, they couldn't say with one hundred percent certainty their ISIS target and the captured aid worker were not there.

Once they'd completed checking the ground floor and upper levels, they started down a set of stairs. These steps weren't finished in the opulent granite tiles of the main level. They were plain concrete, leading to a steel door, heavily reinforced.

Montana took the lead again, fixed C-4 explosives near the handle and pushed a detonator into the clay-like substance.

Everyone backed up the stairs to the main level and held their hands over their ears.

Montana pressed the detonation button. A dull thump shook the floor beneath his feet. A cloud of dust puffed up the staircase.

Lt. Mike held up a hand. "Let it clear a little." Finally, he lowered his hand and led the way back down the stairs to the door.

It hung open on its hinges, a dark, ragged hole blown through the metal. The entrance led to a tunnel-like hallway with doors on either side. Yellowed, florescent lights flickered in the ceiling. Another door marked the end of the long hallway.

The team split, each clearing the rooms, one at a time. None were locked, but the locking mechanisms were on the outsides of the doors. A chill slithered down the back of Montana's neck, partly because of the coolness in the basement and partly from knowing the sheik had probably used the rooms to incarcerate people. Nothing in any of the rooms indicated the aid worker had been imprisoned there.

At the end of the corridor, the final door was locked. Once again, Montana set the charge, the team hid behind the doors of the cell-like rooms, waiting for the charge to blow. Montana only used enough explosive to dislodge the lock mechanism, no more. He didn't want to destroy the structure of the underground portion of the building and risk trapping his team or causing them injury with the concussion.

"You have a gift." Nacho grinned as he passed Montana and followed Lt. Mike into a much narrower tunnel.

"We're in a tunnel beneath the compound," Lt. Mike said into the two-way radio.

Montana doubted Big Bird would hear on the outside. Where the tunnel would lead, they'd know soon enough. Unfortunately, they wouldn't have a sniper on the other end providing cover for them when they emerged from whatever building.

His gut twisting, his nerves stretched, Montana clenched his weapon, holding it at the ready as he continued forward. If they had any chance of rescuing the aid worker, it had to be soon. ISIS rebels had a habit of torturing and killing anyone they could use as an example, rather than hanging on to them. Prisoners only slowed the attack and hampered their determination to take everything in their paths.

The tunnel opened into the bowels of what appeared to be a warehouse.

"I feel like we're on a wild goose chase," Swede muttered.

"And the goose is leading us to the slaughter. Not the other way around," Irish concurred.

They climbed a set of stairs to a huge, empty room.

"Damn," Swede said and bent to a dark lump on the ground.

Nacho released a string of profanity in Spanish.

"We've found the aid worker."

What Montana had assumed was a pile of rags, was in fact a woman, her clothes torn, her body ravaged, her face battered. Her eyes were wide open, staring up at the ceiling.

Swede knelt beside her and touched his fingers to the base of her throat.

Montana's stomach roiled at the sight of the woman's damaged body. He could have told Swede she was already dead. What a waste of life. And for what? "We need to get out of here."

The sound of footsteps made Montana glance up. A man stood on a catwalk twenty feet above them. He shouted something in Pashtu, ending in *Allah*, pulled the pin on a grenade and tossed it into the middle of the team.

"Fuck!" Montana yanked his weapon around and shot the man. He fell to the ground, but killing him was a little too late.

The grenade rolled toward Swede, still crouched beside the woman's body.

"Get down!" Lt. Mike shouted, and then threw himself over the grenade.

Montana shouted, "No!" as the grenade exploded beneath their leader.

The force of the concussion reverberated throughout the room, knocking Montana to the ground. His last thoughts were of the home and the girl he'd once loved.

ABOUT THE AUTHOR

ELLE JAMES also writing as MYLA JACKSON is a *New York Times* and *USA Today* Bestselling author of books including cowboys, intrigues and paranormal adventures that keep her readers on the edges of their seats. With over eighty works in a variety of sub-genres and lengths she has published with Harlequin, Samhain, Ellora's Cave, Kensington, Cleis Press, and Avon. When she's not at her computer, she's traveling, snow skiing, boating, or riding her ATV, dreaming up new stories.

GoodReads | Newsletter
Or visit her alter ego Myla Jackson at mylajackson.com
Website | Facebook | Twitter | Newsletter

Learn more about Elle James
www.ellejames.com
ellejames@ellejames.com

ALSO BY ELLE JAMES

SEAL's Seduction (#6)

SEAL'S Defiance (#7)

SEAL's Deception (#8)

SEAL's Deliverance (#9)

Ballistic Cowboy

Hot Combat (#1)

Hot Target (#2)

Hot Zone (#3)

Hot Velocity (#4)

Texas Billionaire Club

Tarzan & Janine (#1)

Something To Talk About (#2)

Who's Your Daddy (#3)

Love & War (#4)

Hellfire Series

Hellfire, Texas (#1)

Justice Burning (#2)

Smoldering Desire (#3) TBD

Up in Flames (#4) TBD

Plays with Fire (#5) TBD

Hellfire in High Heels (#6) TBD

Cajun Magic Mystery Series

Voodoo on the Bayou (#1)

Voodoo for Two (#2)

Deja Voodoo (#3)

Cajun Magic Mysteries Books 1-3

Billionaire Online Dating Service

The Billionaire Husband Test (#1)

The Billionaire Cinderella Test (#2)

The Billionaire Bride Test (#3) TBD

The Billionaire Matchmaker Test (#4) TBD

SEAL Of My Own

Navy SEAL Survival

Navy SEAL Captive

Navy SEAL To Die For

Navy SEAL Six Pack

Devil's Shroud Series

Deadly Reckoning (#1)

Deadly Engagement (#2)

Deadly Liaisons (#3)

Deadly Allure (#4)

Deadly Obsession (#5)

Deadly Fall (#6)

Covert Cowboys Inc Series

Triggered (#1)

Taking Aim (#2)

Bodyguard Under Fire (#3)

Cowboy Resurrected (#4)

Navy SEAL Justice (#5)

Navy SEAL Newlywed (#6)

High Country Hideout (#7)

Clandestine Christmas (#8)

Thunder Horse Series

CPSIA information can be obtained
at www.ICGtesting.com
Printed in the USA
FSHW01n2027220618
49732FS